To Gail,

TRUE NORTH

An Arctic Fable

JAYANNE SINDT

Always Follow
true North ☺

Jayanne

Gavin,
Happy Birthday
love
Aunt Nan

Dedicated to all my relations

TABLE OF CONTENTS

FOREWORD

To me, and I dare say to many others who have been honored by Jay's acquaintance, the name, Jayanne Sindt has always been synonymous with the majestic creature, the polar bear. I was excited when I heard that Jay was extending her entertaining children's book *Mato Finds True North,* (beautifully illustrated by Jim Hawks), to a full length novel for young adult readers. After reading the first draft of her novel, I felt that Jayanne had told Mato's story with a sense of integrity to the true nature of the polar bear and to herself, for, although, yes, the story was about the experiences of a family of polar bears, the message of finding one's own moral center and tapping into the spiritual strength necessary to achieve your personal quest was dead on Jayanne. As long as I've known her, for going on twenty years, Jayanne has had an intense spiritual focus and an intuitive sense of her own purpose as well as a devotion to the polar bear that seems to have permeated her very being.

I remember Jay's excitement when she, along with her husband, Jim, were able to realize her long held dream to visit the bears in their natural habitat. Much of what they observed and learned about the contemporary polar bears' existence during that trip to Canada gave verisimilitude to Mato's story. I also chuckle to myself occasionally when I remember Jay's irritation with the Coca Cola marketing venture of 2008 in which polar bears and penguins were graphically depicted sharing a frosty soda - "Don't they know that penguins live in the Southern Hemisphere and polar bears at the Arctic Circle, in the NORTH! They're misinforming the public!" Now, yes, I know, of course, *Mato* is a fictionalized children's story with anthropomorphic beasts - talking cubs and foxes and a Spirit Bear honoring the Creator - but Jayanne's intention to depict, honestly, the contemporary issues experienced by the polar bears in their natural and unnatural habitats is evident in her telling of their story, and her faith in the resiliency of these intelligent creatures was paramount.

Jayanne tends to be passionate about whom and what she loves, but she also has the ability to appreciate and respect the reality of a being and its life without over sentimentality or delusion. She knows polar bears are carnivores and that their primary food source is the ringed or bearded seal, a very adorable creature by any animal lover's standards. She knows that their hunting practice can be violent, ferocious even. Jay acknowledges that the increased melting of the ice flows, caused by whatever reason, is problematic for the already vulnerable species as is the encroaching human presence in the polar bears' habitat. She depicts the somewhat precarious relationship between mankind and the bear, and the types of incidents that might occur due to humans' fear, gluttony or greed. She also depicts the bear in a spiritual light which is so appropriate as they have been revered in numerous shamanistic rituals practiced by numerous indigenous cultures. These reflections of reality run throughout Jayanne's cubs' story.

When I think of Jayanne's life-long devotion to the white bear and this venture here - writing her first Mato story with her illustrator friend, Jim Hawks, attending school class rooms to share her knowledge and appreciation for the bears with the many students, and now her commitment to a full length novel, I am somewhat assured that the Inuit belief that the souls of polar bears and humans are interchangeable is true. The Inuit and Eskimo, like Jayanne, understood that the polar bear was and still is a highly intelligent teacher who closely resembles the human in physiology, diet and nature.

In *Mato's* story, Jayanne is entertaining and educating her readers without scaring or saddening them or moralizing or blaming. She BELIEVES in the bear's innate ability to find their way and to adapt and survive. She has chosen to believe in the resiliency of her beloved *Ursus maritimus,* and the innate desire of humanity, and the universe, to follow their True North.

By Jeannie Evans-Boniecki, PhD

Sometimes a dead end
Is just a moment to make a choice
Survey the situation
And listen to your inner voice

When you are troubled or confused
And don't know how to move forth
Trust in your own direction
And head for True North

-Jayanne

CHAPTER ONE

THE RACE TO SEA

"I win, I win!" Mato (*MAH-toe*) heaved his thousand-pound body up onto an ice sheet. Standing on all four paws, he shook, spraying seawater everywhere. In victory, he reached upward, rose onto his two hind legs, and shouted, "I'm the first to hit the open water! I win."

He had finally beaten Ursula, his much smaller sister, across the pack ice on the way to the open sea. It was the annual ending of winter; it was spring on the Arctic ice cap. The polar bear cub siblings have raced across the pack ice to the open water ever since they were a year old and large enough to swim. Then their mother joined them to swim the long distance from the Arctic ice to the tundra of Canada.

Each year Mato started out in the lead, but Ursula always overtook him on the pack ice. She was far more agile and quick, jumping from one wobbly sheet to another with the precision and grace of a ballerina dancing. Mato was sloppy and cumbersome. He had to slow down to keep his balance while navigating the tilting sheets of ice.

But this year, Mato's size had doubled compared to his sister's, and his extended stride made up for his lack of agility. He practically jumped across two ice sheets at a time, not noticing only about a hundred yards of pack ice. This was only a tenth of the distance they usually raced. So, he stayed in front until the finish. Ursula was a mere two sheets of ice away. Mato remained standing on his hind legs with his front paws crossed and resting on his chest, tapping his back paw as if to say, "What took you so long?" This became the young male polar bear's proudest moment, next to hunting his first seal alone.

Ursula scolded him while making her last strides, "Jumping in before the chunks end doesn't count. Mato, I have to tell you every time! You have to get all the way…"

Ursula remained on all fours and stretched her nose over the water, trying to catch a scent. Many things passed through her mind. She was attentive because she would soon be caring for cubs of her own, a much larger responsibility than just hunting for oneself. Occupied by her many thoughts, she completely ignored Mato, and turned around to greet their approaching mother.

Mato dropped his front paws and plopped to all fours, "What? Do not even try to say that I didn't win!" He paced the few steps the narrow sheet would allow, causing the seawater to slosh.

Their mother approached and surveyed the abruptly ending pack ice.

"Nana?" With that one word, Ursula asked her mother many questions. What happened to the pack ice? Are they going to swim back to the tundra? How is it possible that Mato can win without cheating?

Nana returned her gaze for a moment, then ambled up beside Mato and extended her nose like her daughter. Mato stood still. Along with Ursula's many questions, Nana had other things on her mind. This was much more than an ending of winter on the Arctic ice cap. Maybe that's why she waited an extra week to make the big swim, to stay with her cubs longer. For Nana, this was the last of many things. These two cubs were the last of her litters.

Mato could not remain still any longer, "I am at the end!" He protested. "See—*no more ice*! You cannot say I didn't get here first! I didn't even cheat this time!" He stomped a front paw by the edge knocking a large chunk of ice into the open water. All three bears had to steady themselves on the rocking ice sheet.

Nana turned away to hide her smirk from Mato. "Too far to swim," she said matter-of-factly as she walked back toward the solid ice shore.

"But I won…" complained Mato.

"Nobody won, stupid!" Ursula scolded. Her brother's lack of observation annoyed her once again. "Don't you see that we are here *way* too soon? The pack ice should go on for *at least* another mile!"

Mato looked to the ice shore, and then at the open sea again. He seemed to deflate as he bowed his head. He then nodded to Ursula. Mato wondered what life would be like without his sister to explain things to him. As they moved from one ice sheet to another, he grumbled to Ursula, "I just thought I got lucky when the pack ice ended before you could catch and pass me. More swimming is good, isn't it?"

Ursula stopped. She wondered how life would be for Mato without her there to explain things. "Mato, don't you pay attention to *anything* Nana says? You won't have her *or* me to rely on when you are on your own. You really should—"

"Yeah, yeah, spare me the lecture, my dear sister, and just *answer the question*. We always swim, and we swim far—no problem."

Ursula sighed, and then explained yet another thing to her brother, "Even the strongest swimmers can be challenged by a regular trip back to the tundra in spring to spend the summer.

Every year, the distance has been getting farther and farther. Some smaller bears or those that haven't eaten well like us can even drown before they reach land."

They started walking again.

"It hasn't really been that much trouble for me," Mato shrugged.

"We're not all as big and buoyant as you are!" Ursula retorted.

Mato stopped and raised himself up on his hind legs. He extended his chest to its widest expanse and playfully exclaimed, "And you shall fear the Mighty Mato!"

Ursula stopped. "Yeah right," she sneered. "You know I can still kick your butt." She started walking.

Mato dropped to all fours and looked around, knowing his sister was right. Even with his much larger size, she could out-think, outrun, and outwrestle him any day. He quickly changed the subject from his much smaller sister's prowess, "Hey, have you seen Chuck?"

"You know he hates it when you call him that," Ursula commented.

"Yeah, so? You and Nana call him Charlie," said Mato.

"Well, he likes *us*," she faked a British accent, "You, on the other hand, Master Mato, are quite annoying." Mato chuckled as Ursula continued, "Young man bear, your manners are appalling. I prefer to be acknowledged by my proper name— Charles. I am from a long line of foxes, you know, dating back to the hunted red foxes of England. 'Chuck' is nothing short of a mongrel term."

Mato laughed, "What is a mongrel anyway?"

"There he is, talking to Nana." Ursula pointed with her nose.

Nana stood with a tiny creature, about the size of small dog. Charles, the arctic fox, had pointy ears and a fluffy white tail. Although arctic foxes can have great feasts on the scraps polar bears leave behind, the animals usually did not mix. The bears tolerated Charles and did not attack him, even in lean times. The cubs knew that Nana found Charles to be quite resourceful. Nana sniffed toward the ocean as her children approached. The fox greeted them with a tiny bow.

Nana sighed, "Well, my grown ones, it looks like you'll be in my company a bit longer. These are strange times, and I am reluctant to send you on your own just yet." She smiled inside and knew that she would have some more time with them, even though they were ready to be on their own.

"Nana," Ursula asked, "will this ice sustain us for summer?"

Nana gazed out to sea, extending her nose, "Perhaps," she then set her eyes on her children, "Perhaps," she repeated as she began walking. Mato and Ursula followed.

Charles trotted beside at a comfortable distance, so as not to be trampled by or become a sudden snack for these polar bears. Although he and Nana had been friends for a long time, he knew that a polar bear could find him to be a tiny treat at any moment. And, though he relied on these bears for his meals, he knew he should not fully trust them. After all, a hungry male polar bear would even eat a polar bear cub if hungry enough. Surely, a friendly fox could be on a carnivore's menu.

Charles addressed Nana, "A fox friend tells me that it is the same all over the Arctic ice cap. He had been with a Siberian group of polar bears on the other side of the ice cap and was hoping to have better luck there. They can't pick up a scent of Siberian tundra either."

Nana nodded and blinked at Charles.

"Hey thanks for the good news, *Chuck*," Mato teased.

Charles responded by sticking his nose pointedly into the air and changing his trot to a prance.

Mato laughed.

"One day, Mato," Nana began, "You will learn to appreciate the fox. He is a great resource, not merely entertainment." She felt this would be a good time for a gentle reminder, even though she knew Mato was only teasing.

Mato bowed his head, "Yes ma'am." Mato did not care about giving respect to an animal that might be an easy snack, but he was certain to respect his mother. She taught him everything he knew about survival. Also, he had his sister to remind him about everything. He still did not quite understand the usefulness of the fox, but decided he would now consider the fox's contributions since Nana had mentioned them several times.

The four continued walking. Mato wondered when the next hunt would be.

CHAPTER TWO

AMONG MALES

With Charles trotting ahead to scout, the polar bears continued walking toward the center of the Arctic ice cap. Nana stopped and whiffed a scent. Mato and Ursula copied. They could smell male polar bears, at least two or three, but maybe more.

Mato begged, "Please, Nana, let me go check them out—I'm going to be around other males soon enough without my mom and sister. Plus, I'm really big now…" Mato began to stand up on his hind legs.

Nana waved him down. In his disappointment, Mato bowed on all fours and started to sway his head from side to side while leaning from one front paw to the other. He mumbled to himself, "I never get to do anything I want to do."

Nana contemplated letting her cub venture alone among the male bears. Females with cubs always stayed away from male bears. Without cubs, they only allowed males to approach during mating season in the spring. Mato was unusually large for his age and she felt that his size alone might deter them from attempting to confront him. Yet she was more comforted knowing that she and Ursula would be nearby. They were much smaller females, but quite formidable. Joining the other males would be a good test for the young male soon to be on his own.

"Follow your True North, Mato," Nana said.

Mato was so busy mumbling about never getting to do anything that he didn't hear his mother. He continued to sway his head.

Ursula hollered at Mato, "She *said*, 'Follow your True North,' you big galoot!"

Mato stopped moving and looked up. His mother slowly closed her eyes while bowing her head ever so slightly. Mato's eyes widened and darted quickly from his sister to his mother. He knew what Nana meant by "follow your True North." It meant to listen to his heart, and he had a strong desire to approach the males. He was eager to meet male bears like himself and he felt drawn to the other males. He poked his nose up into the air and headed into the direction of the male bears.

Beyond a hard packed snowy ridge, he saw a gathering of male polar bears. There was a group of three, another two nearby, and one other bear pacing by himself. "Wow," thought Mato, "six males!"

Nana and Ursula followed Mato for several yards, and stayed on the ridge within scent but out of sight. Ursula was concerned for her brother, "Nana, there are so many, do you think he'll be OK?"

"My valiant Ursula, you can outperform any one of those bears." Nana reassured her. Ursula blushed as Nana turned to look upon the males. "We can easily help Mato with all of those bears, if necessary." Nana confirmed.

Mato ambled along with his most casual stride. He broadened his shoulders, lifted his back, and held his head steady, muttering to himself, "I'm a big ol' bear and I'll mosey over here and I'll mosey over there, because I'm a big ol' bear that can go anywhere without a care…"

Mato decided to approach the single pacing bear to warm up. This bear was average height, but skinny. As Mato approached, he saw a figure eight pattern that the bear had paced into the ice. Mato concluded that the bear had been pacing for a long time, days even. The bear's coat had a strange glimmer to it and he smelled odd, not like an animal or fish scent. Mato could hear the bear talking to himself.

The bear did not notice Mato. He was involved with his pacing and the conversation with himself, "Sure, no sweat dude, you can do it, yeah dude, get back, get the goods, swim dude, find it, the dumps, dude, that's where it's at, the dumps, dude, got the best stuff."

Just as Mato was about to speak, the bear stopped pacing, whirled around on his hind legs, held up his front paws in protest toward Mato, and said, "It wasn't me dude, I didn't use no PCBs, dude. Don't lay that human rap on me, dude. I just get the good stuff, you know, from the dump…" He moved backward on his hind legs as Mato approached.

Mato shook his head, "What are you talking about? What's a dump? What's a human? And what in the world is a PCB?"

The bear looked around frantically, held a paw up to his snout, "Shh, shh, dude! Not so loud, don't be tellin' all these other bears about the good stuff dude—"

Mato became annoyed, "Hey, *dude*, I have no idea what you are talking about!" Mato sniffed at the bear, "Are you even a polar bear?"

The bear relaxed, "Aw, dude, yeah. I'm a polar bear! It's cool, be cool." He held out a paw for Mato to shake, "Name's Slick."

Mato tapped Slick's paw with his own, "Mato."

"Mato, that sounds Eskimo, you Indian?" Slick asked.

"I don't know," Mato shrugged. "Nana gave me the name."

"Nana? You mean your momma! Hey, you are really big, but you're just a baby bear, aren't you?" Slick started sniffing around, "Where is your momma at?"

"I am *not* a baby," Mato demanded as he rose up on his hind legs to his full height, "I'm *grown!*" He growled.

"Hee, hee, hee" Slick chuckled with a raspy inhale holding his belly with one paw as he leaned into Mato, "I'm just playin' with you, dude, just playin'. I'm Alaskan, and got my name from the Big Spill." He dropped to all fours.

"Oh," Mato slowly moved down to all fours. He wondered where Alaska was and what the "Big Spill" meant. "Well, then, nice to meet you. I'm from Canada. I really don't understand a lot of what you are talking about."

"Canadian, humph. No worries, babe, I mean, *big bear* about what I was sayin' before." He tilted his head in the direction of the group of three bears. "Don't look, but them boys over there are Canadian too. At least one of them is. They all did time in Churchill together and have been hanging out ever since."

"Churchill?"

"Yeah, dude, Churchill, in Canada, by the bay, good hunting— and a good dump too. The trouble is too many humans. They put you in bear jail if you get too close."

Mato began to wonder if this bear was from another planet. This Slick was using so many words he had never heard before. He was having a lot of trouble following the conversation. He tried a different approach, "Are you going to Alaska for summer?"

Slick started pacing again. "Dude, that be the thing, dude," he kept his pace to a few steps and continued chatting with Mato, "Shoot, the ice left too soon, man. Too far to swim!" He waved his front paws and dropped to all fours. "I ain't been home since the Big Spill! Can't get to any dumps! No dumps up here—need land and humans for dumps." His pace began to widen as he returned to his figure eight and muttered to himself.

Mato nodded a farewell to Slick and headed in the direction of the other bears. Slick just might be the strangest bear he had ever met. He decided to work his way up to the "Churchill boys" and approached the two bears next.

As Mato approached, the two bears wrestled. When he was within a few strides, they stopped to watch him, stood up on two legs, and leaned against each other.

"Oh my, look at this strapping young bear there, ya, Lars?"

"Oh, ya, Sven, such big paws he has."

"And, ooh what a big head…" Sven smacked Lars with his free paw alongside the head.

"What?!" Lars held his head.

Sven continued, "Lars, we haven't been introduced."

Hearing their conversation, Mato felt awkward. He did not recognize their Danish accent, having never heard bears talk like this before. The bears separated, walked upright around each side of Mato and looked him over—up and down. Their front paws hung limply at the wrists as they walked rather lightly on two legs.

"I am Sven", said Sven

"And I am Lars," said Lars

"We are from Greenland," they shouted together.

"We are *not* from Denmark though our accents sound that way." Sven explained.

"GREENLAND" They both shouted.

"Okay" said Mato, "I get it, you are from Greenland."

"We see you have met our Slick, ya?" said Lars from Mato's left.

"A very interesting fellow, ya?" chimed Sven from Mato's right.

Mato turned his head slowly toward one bear while trying to see the other out of the corner of his eye, "Ya, I mean, *yeah*," stammered Mato.

Meanwhile, Nana and Ursula looked on from their safe distance. Ursula did not like the way the two males were moving around her brother. She bristled and started to rise up on her hind legs.

"Down, girl," whispered Nana, "He is doing better than expected. See how he does not react to their advances?" Ursula deflated and growled soft and low.

Sven and Lars finished circling Mato and met back together in front of him. Mato made a nod in the direction of Slick and asked, "What's a dump?"

"Oooh," Sven's eyes rolled upward as he lifted the back of his front paw to his forehead falling into the arms of Lars, "So big, so white, and so innocent. Oh, the things I can *show* you, young bear!" Lars gave Sven a little shove and Sven hopped back to his hind legs.

"Silly, ya?" Lars looked at Sven then to Mato, "Dump. The dump is no good—very bad for bears."

Sven stepped forward talking to Mato, "Sure, ya, it *tastes* good and all of that," then he stepped back from Mato, "but is no good for *body*." Sven moved his front paws over his chest and hips as he said body.

"Is that because of the PCB?" Mato queried further.

"Ya, ya—all the human scraps in dump—it makes bad food for bears." Lars jumped in, "PCB bad for body—humans make it."

"What is a human?" Mato asked.

Sven and Lars answer interchangeably with Lars first, "They say he melts the ice."

"And makes the oil slick."

"And kills the food."

"And raises the temperature—"

Mato interrupted, "Humans must be huge—great and powerful creatures!"

Sven and Lars looked at each other, then back at Mato, and busted out laughing. They laughed wildly and uncontrollably—dropped to their knees first, and then rolled around one another. Mato waved a paw at them in dismissal and walked away on all fours.

Nana and Ursula continued to watch. Ursula started a whisper, "Without getting any bigger—"

Nana finished, "He has them rolling onto their backs."

Together they said, "Unbelievable," shaking their heads in disbelief.

"Ah," said Nana as she watched Mato approach the group of three bears, "Here is the real test."

The three bears, situated in relaxed poses, did not stir as Mato approached. "They are quite still," Nana noted. Ursula growled low and soft again.

As Mato moseyed toward the three bears, he cleared his throat to alert them of his presence. One of the bears was sitting with his back against a block of snow and ice. Even while sitting he appeared as large as Mato. Another smaller bear was curled up on the ground. The third bear, about the same size as Mato, lay faced away from Mato. The third bear spoke, without moving, "Now, what did you say to get those Danes laughing so hard? Not that it takes much to make them, ahem, joyous."

Mato paused, "Who—me?"

The reclined bear raised his eyebrow.

Realizing that the reclined bear was speaking to him, "Oh, I asked them a question," Mato replied.

The seated bear slid to his side, resting his head on his elbow, "Must have been a very funny question, no?" He looked at Mato with wonder. This accent Mato recognized, Charles had mimicked it once when describing Siberia.

"What did you ask?" The small bear uncurled himself while addressing Mato.

"Well," Mato bowed his head, swaying from front paw to paw, "First I asked what a dump is…"

13

"OK," said the small bear, "so you haven't gotten around much…" The other bears didn't stir.

"Then," Mato continued, "I asked what a human is…"

"Definitely have not gotten around much," the small bear confirmed.

"What is so funny then? What did you say to make the Dane bears roll around laughing?" asked the very large bear looking up from his elbow.

Mato rocked faster from paw to paw mumbling, "Well, those bears kept going on and on about what humans do…" he lifted his head looking at the very large bear, "so I said this human must be a huge and great creature."

The reclined bear chuckled without moving. The very large bear and the small bear looked at each other. Mato stopped rocking and stood, bewildered. The reclined bear sniffed the air. "Big, but very young, I think I smell your momma, boy."

Mato made himself bigger, "I am a grown bear and on my own!"

The very large bear sat up, "Really?"

Mato returned his gaze fiercely, "Really! My Nana has taught me well—"

The small bear hopped up on two feet, "Did you say Nana?"

Mato began to lift up his front paws, preparing to stand up on two legs, "Who's asking?"

"Nana," the small bear persisted, "as in *Na-nuq-a*? (*Na-NOOK-ah*)"

Now Mato stood on his hind legs and began to make himself appear larger, "I said, who is asking?"

Nana and Ursula inched forward, completely stealth, but getting larger in size. They prepared to assist Mato if necessary.

On his hind legs, the small bear was as high as Mato's shoulder. "Easy there, big boy, I'm Oslo, the big guy is Ket, and Big Al is relaxing, like you should be."

Ket looked from one to the other, "Nanuqa she is a legendary bear, great hunter, and the best nose. All the bears in Churchill speak of her."

Mato dropped his front paws, "Really?"

Oslo explains, "This Nana, you say she's your momma, if she's Nanuqa, she is the greatest female ever to wander the ice. All our mommas told us about her, and all our brothers speak of her."

"Even in my country, Siberia" Ket nodded.

"And Norway," Oslo agreed.

"And Churchill," Al continued. "Even those goofy Danes from Greenland know about your momma, boy. I'm surprised she didn't explain this stuff to you." He shifted onto his back, slightly tightening his front paws across his chest.

Mato flopped to a seated position with his back legs straight and his front paws plopped in between. His head shook back and forth, "I never even heard about humans until I talked with that Slick bear over there." With his head, he motioned toward Slick.

Nana and Ursula slid back and wondered about Mato's submissive behavior.

"She didn't tell me anything about PCBs, dumps, Churchill, doing time *or* Danes from Greenland." He looked at his front paws.

"As for the Danes from Greenland, well that is a long story about bears from Denmark settling in Greenland, and Greenland claiming its independence" Oslo said.

With his mouth open, Mato stared at Oslo.

Nana and Ursula looked at each other. Ursula asked, "Nana, are males always this chatty?"

"You have no idea," Nana replied.

"Ah" Ket explained, "Churchill is a place—"

"Where we all have done time," Oslo finished.

"Thanks to those human creatures," Al added.

"How do you *do time*?" Mato asked.

Oslo stood up, but remained cautious of Mato. He moved around as he proceeded. "Churchill is a place with a great dump and a whole village of humans…The dump is their scrap pile—"

Ket jumped in before Mato could ask, "Human is a small creature. Not so small as fox, but small, and with two legs." He nodded at Oslo to continue.

Oslo nodded back to Ket, "And the humans don't like when you get too close to their village. They think we want to eat them."

Ket shook his head, "Ugh, too bony!"

Al chuckled.

Oslo proceeded, "So, they point a stick at us and hit us with this thing that pinches and makes it like you are sleeping," he stood as though he were aiming a rifle.

"But still awake." Ket interjected.

"Yeah," continued Oslo, moving in slow motion. "You can see, sort of, but all your parts are sleeping and you can't move." Oslo dropped to the ground and lay there, wide-eyed and motionless.

"Anyway," Ket rolled his eyes.

Oslo hopped back up, "Anyway, so, if you get too close to town, they point this stick at you, you feel a pinch, you kind of sleep, and, before you know it, you're being hauled off to bear jail!"

Al added from his repose, "The big tin den."

Oslo paced on his hind legs gesturing with his front paws, "Where they keep you and give you water until the whirlybird comes—"

Mato asked, "Whirlybird?"

"Yes, whirlybird," Ket repeated, "A human machine that flies like bird."

Becoming more animated, Oslo said, "Yeah, yeah, the whirlybird. And the humans pinch you again to make you sleepy, strap you into a blanket, lift you in the air, and put you down about thirty miles away from Churchill, which is actually cool because you get a big start on the ice for hunting." Then he sat down.

Al uncrossed his front paws and placed them behind his head like a pillow, "A free ride to the hunting ice."

"Ha! Too scary, even for free, I don't like it." Ket shook his head.

Oslo blankly stared at the ice in front of him, "And the tin den is soooo boring."

"Yeah," Al settled into his new pose, "nothing like doing time in Churchill."

Mato awoke from his open-mouthed and dumbfounded stupor and said, "We—I mean *I* was looking to swim to the tundra but I couldn't even get a scent of it across the water…"

"Why do you think we're hanging out here…?" Oslo gestured toward Slick and the Danes, "with all these other bears?"

Al pondered, "It actually reminds me of Churchill before winter, waiting for the ice to come."

Mato hiked his hind legs underneath and sat upright, "Do you think the humans can come here in whirlybirds, pinch us, and take us to the tundra?"

Oslo and Ket laughed.

Al finally sat up. "Ya know something kid, you might have something there. Except, Churchill is the only place I know that moves bears around like that and only because we were so close to humans."

Ket said, "No humans here, no."

"Hey. *Hey*, what about those guys way in the center of the ice with those big foxes?" Oslo interjected.

Ket corrected, "Not foxes, dogs."

"Yeah, whatever, those humans use the dogs to move around," Oslo said.

Al lay down again on his back, putting his front paws behind his head again, "That's North Pole station."

Oslo clapped his front paws together, "The Pole, that's it, they have whirlybirds there."

Al contradicted, "Not to move bears. And, they used a boat to bring the whirlybird."

Mato asked, "What's a boat?"

Oslo replied, "The human's machine for water, they got machines for everything, whirlybirds to fly, boats to move on water. They even have machines to move across the snow and ice…"

Mato asked, "Dogs?"

Oslo replied, "No, well, yeah, dogs pull them but they also have these smelly, noisy machines that go way faster."

"Relax, kid," Al counseled. "Chill out here with the rest of us, we're not the only warm blood around here. There is still plenty to go around."

Mato sighed and stood up, "Thanks anyway, but it's time for me to move on. You sure have given me a lot to think about!" On all fours, he began to mosey away.

Oslo, "Have it your way, kid."

Ket nodded.

"And say hello to your Nana for us," Al chuckled, motionless again.

Mato paused for a moment and considered protesting Al, but shook his head and continued on his way. He went in the opposite direction from where Nana and Ursula watched.

CHAPTER THREE

STRANGE TIMES

Mato continued to mosey away from the males. His mother and sister moved a couple of hundred yards away from where they watched Mato interact with the male polar bears. They had agreed earlier to a meeting spot downwind of where the male bears were. Mato was to appear to be on his own, not backtracking to meet with someone. Yet Nana was certain that she and her daughter had been detected. Mato noticed Charles trotting alongside him, a few feet away. Mato nodded toward Charles, and then hung his head. He was trying to process all this new information from the males.

Charles trotted in a bit closer, "Why so glum, grown Mato? You just engaged one, then two, and then *three* male bears at a time. I should think you'd be whistling a merry tune."

Mato stopped, "Chuck, can I ask you a question?"

Charles stopped and sat down, "You may." He inched a bit closer to Mato.

"Why didn't Nana tell us about all the stuff I just heard? Why didn't she tell us about dumps, and humans, and whirlybirds, and—"

Charles gently interrupted, "And the fact that your dear Nana is the most legendary huntress ever to grace the Arctic Circle, known as the fearless and cunning Nanuqa?

Mato lifted his head up and, looking with sad eyes at Charles, said, "Yeah." Mato held back tears.

Charles could see Mato felt betrayed. He explained, "Nana has spoken with me about this very thing. She wanted you and your sister to know the life she has known. She wanted to show you a world without humans. More importantly, she wants you to be known for your own accomplishments, not hers."

Mato dropped his head and sniffled, "It still would have been nice to hear this stuff from her."

"Ah, my grown Mato, let it be the voices of others to tell you such things. Let your mother's voice be that of all the wisdom you need to rely on when on your own."

This annoyed Mato. He looked up quickly and snapped, "How can I use wisdom with things I've never seen or even heard of before?"

Charles jumped back a few inches, "Some answers can only be found within your own experience."

Mato started walking again. Charles followed at a safe distance.

Unable to contain herself, Ursula ran at full speed and leapt up to give Mato a high five. Mato reluctantly raised his paw to meet hers. Still excited, but now showing concern, Ursula asked, "What's the matter with you, *big* brother? You were awesome down there! Like the big *man* bear stirring up all the lesser bears." Mato grunted.

Nana approached, "You have done well, my grown son." Mato couldn't look at Nana. She looked at Charles who motioned for her to come away to chat. Nana and Charles walked a few feet away while Ursula play punched her bigger brother. "So, what did they say, huh, Mato? What did the good old boys have to say?"

Mato flopped to a seated position, his head still down. "Stuff that Nana never told us, stuff that *you* don't even know." Ursula stopped punching him and sat next to him.

"Wanna talk about it, bro?" she asked, nudging Mato.

Mato sighed and began to share with his sister.

Meanwhile, Nana chatted with Charles, "I see he has been informed about many, many things, including me."

"Yes, my lady, things he wishes to have heard from you," Charles informed her.

Nana looked over at her children, "Perhaps he is correct. Better to be informed."

"What does your heart tell you?" Charles asked.

"My heart says that these are strange times." Nana said.

"That they are, my dear lady. That they are," Charles agreed. "I must tell all of you about some information I got from that fox friend who traveled with a Siberian bear."

"Let's rejoin the children." Nana said, moving away from Charles.

As Nana and Charles walked back toward the younger bears, Ursula shouted, "I always knew you were a legend, Nana! I don't need some jailhouse Churchill bear to tell me that." She nuzzled Nana.

"But Mato would rather I had told him." Nana lifted Mato's head with her nose and looked deep into his eyes.

Mato caught a glimpse of his mother's gaze then stood up to get some distance. He shook his head, and looked at his mother. "Please Nana, I don't mean any disrespect. It's just that, well, I mean, approaching those males as if I owned the place looked silly when I didn't even know what language they were speaking and using words I had never even heard before, you know? I just think it would have been easier on my stomach if…"

Nana moved closer to Mato, still gazing at him, "If I had told you sooner." She finished for him. Mato sat back down and met his mother's gaze. "In these strange times, I am inclined to think that you may be right." Nana added.

Mato's jaw dropped, "Did you just say I may be right?"

Nana smiled, "Indeed you may."

Mato fell onto his back and moved his limbs like making a snow angel. He reveled in her words that he repeated over and over, "I may be right, I may be right, Nana says I may be right…"

Nana and Ursula looked at each other, rolled their eyes, and walked away from Mato.

As loudly as he could, Charles cleared his throat, "Ahem, *ahem*, I have some very important and interesting things to tell all of you, speaking of strange times."

Nana and Ursula turned toward Charles and sat down. Mato continued mumbling about may be being right. Ursula reached over to smack him. Mato stuck his big black tongue out at her.

Charles pranced back and forth as he spoke, "I've discovered that there is an Alaskan Bear, just due north of here. He seems to know things about the strange ice thaw and odd movements of the pack ice. He also may be able to explain the increase in humans as he claims they quest for something called black gold.

He is not exactly an arctic polar bear. Though his white color is similar to yours, he is not really designed for cold and he has a shape more closely related to the grizzly bear. They say that he is very wise to the ways of the changing world."

"You mean the melting world," Ursula said sarcastically.

"Whatever it is called," Nana said, "we must learn to adapt to our world, however it changes, if we are to survive. Ursula needs to know how to be a mother in this new world, as do her daughters, and their daughters."

Mato grumbled.

Ursula snapped at him, "Boys are such babies. They have no idea about the responsibility of keeping a lineage. All you care about is filling your belly and how big you can get."

"Yeah, well, all you care about is filling your belly and raising cubs," Mato retorted.

Charles and Nana laughed loudly.

Ursula and Mato stopped bickering and simultaneously asked, "*What*?"

Nana stopped laughing and said, "You are both important for survival."

"Raising cubs is harder." Ursula snorted.

"Yeah, raising *you*," Mato chided. Ursula stood up to smack him.

Charles shouted, "*Anyway!* If I may continue…I thought we might journey to see this white bear and get some information."

Nana explained, "It will be good to get any information we can. So, instead of by sea, we shall journey by ice. Lead the way, Charlie."

Charles bowed, and headed inland toward the North Pole.

CHAPTER FOUR

A WILD RIDE

The bears and the arctic fox proceeded inland. The terrain of snow and ice pack was changing. Crevasses—enormously deep cracks in the ice—had formed, sloping downward on ridges. Some crevasses were wide expanses, while others were narrow enough to leap across. The depth of some crevasses appeared bottomless. Some had melting ice rushing through in torrents of water. These looked like ice waterfalls under the surface.

The group reached the top of a ridge keeping a slow and steady pace. They stopped near a cornice—a formation of wind-blown, packed snow extending over a ridge. The cornice jutted out ten feet over the edge. There was a jagged looking crevasse below it.

Charles, being lighter, looked over the edge of the crevasse and surveyed the area for a safe passage to the ice valley below. Mato, not paying attention to his own size and weight, moved stealthily up behind Charles intending to startle him.

"Hey, Chuck!" Mato shouted.

Crack! As Charles turned to look at Mato, the entire cornice slab began to break away from the ridgeline. It landed on the ice below and slid toward the crevasse, like a runaway toboggan, with its two passengers.

Nana and Ursula had stepped back from the edge at the sound of the crack. They quickly and carefully searched for a passage around to the crevasse that Mato and Charles would soon be sliding into. They could hear Charles yelling, "Maaaatooooooooooooo!"

Mato and Charles slid on their ice chunk toboggan for almost seventy-five feet before dropping into the crevasse. As they plummeted into the enormous opening, their ice-chunk toboggan fell away. Mato reached out to grab Charles by his tail. Mato landed on his butt and continued to slide along a ledge on the inside wall of the underground cliff of the crevasse. While holding Charles with a front paw, Mato put his hind paws out in front to stop them on the ledge. As they came to a stop, Charles dangled by his tail over the dark emptiness of the crevasse that went to unknown depths below.

"M-m-m master Mato, c-careful now…" Charles stuttered as Mato slowly moved the fox over himself and onto the ledge. Charles scurried toward the inner wall of the crevasse and Mato slowly rolled onto his belly to join his companion. Charles shuddered and tried to steady his breath.

"Scared ya, didn't I?" Mato teased.

Charles sighed loudly before beginning his lecture, "Although your heroics of grabbing me from the abyss were impressive, I don't appreciate your little game that began our predicament in the first place! Really, Master Mato, this is no laughing matter. You and I came as close as anyone to our demise!"

Mato shrugged, "Bad luck, eh, Chuck?"

Charles shook himself, giving special attention to his tail. "The name is Charles." He turned away to look down the ledge. "This ledge seems to go on farther. You better let me have a go at it."

"I'll be right here, Chuck." Mato replied, settling in to relax on his belly.

Nana and Ursula reached the edge of the crevasse. Ursula hollered into the darkness from above, "Mato! Charlie!"

Mato looked upward where daylight shone into the massive ice crack, "Down here, all safe, OK, no one is hurt, Chuck is getting us out of here…"

Nana looked at Ursula and pondered, "Well, we know Charlie can get out, but our Mato is quite large…"

Charles trotted back along the ledge to Mato, "Listen carefully, Master Mato, stay very close to the wall and follow me s-l-o-w-l-y." Mato, still on his belly with his front paws to his side, propelled himself slowly forward with his hind legs, almost slithering along the wall. Overheated polar bears often take this pose to cool off. Mato was certainly feeling overheated after their wild ride.

Above, Nana and Ursula followed the crack as it became narrower and stopped where the crack ended.

Below, Charles remained two feet in front of Mato jumping up and down to test the ledge, Mato chuckled, "Chuck, do you really think that will make a difference?"

Charles stopped jumping, "I suppose you are correct. I weigh about as much as one of your front paws!" They proceeded to where the opening above narrowed and the ceiling got lower. Luckily, the ledge inclined upward toward the surface. Charles could see a strong beam of light about six feet above the ledge, which also grew narrower, "Stay very, very close to the wall, Master Mato!"

Above, Nana and Ursula took turns peering into the narrow end of the ice crack. "I can hear them getting closer!" exclaimed Ursula as she positioned herself to pounce the opening as though breaking through the ice to capture a seal pup.

"Wait!" cautioned Nana. She put her paw on Ursula's shoulder as Ursula backed down. "Let Charles clear it first so we know where to pounce."

The ledge narrowed to about six feet near the end where it closed up on the surface. Charles, now about ten feet away, called, "Ladies, might that be you on the surface?"

"Indeed we are," responded Ursula in her fake British accent.

"Jolly good," Charles replied. "Now give that crack a poke just at the end of it for us if you would be so kind."

Ursula looked at Nana, who nodded the OK. Ursula pounded around the hole as if she hadn't eaten in weeks and was about to dine on seal.

Mato slid up to Charles who had stayed back to avoid the falling ice and snow. Using her head and shoulders, Ursula peered into her newly crafted hole. "Are you coming or what?"

"Right away, Miss Ursula." Charles turned to Mato, "May I please have some assistance?"

"The pleasure is mine," Mato replied as he slowly stood up, moved closer to the opening, and ever so gingerly lifted Charles up through to the surface.

"Now stay right where you are, Master Mato!" Charles called down.

Mato leaned against the wall trying not to look down into the darkness beyond the few feet left to the ledge. "No problem."

Charles directed Nana and Ursula to back up along the surface crack and break through the snowpack a couple of feet to the other side of Mato where the ledge was a couple of feet wider. In seconds, the skilled females had created a Mato-sized hole.

"It's as if I were leaving the den." Mato joked as he climbed to the surface. Nana and Ursula rolled their eyes. "Hey, Chuck," Mato started, "I mean, well, excuse me, Charles."

"Yes, Master Mato?" Charles replied.

"Sorry, and thank you," Mato said sheepishly.

"Don't mention it and no worries," Charles smiled. "And, well, thank *you*, Master Mato for finally using my proper name."

All became aware of Nana sniffing the air. They looked toward the North Pole and saw a strange, colorful cloud that seemed to rise from the surface of the ice.

"I think we may have stumbled upon a shortcut," Charles said.

Nana began walking in the direction of the colorful cloud and the rest followed. As they got closer to the cloud, they could see that it was rising up from a triangular structure. As they approached, the cloud changed color.

"Why are northern lights coming out of that thing?" asked Mato.

"If I were to venture a guess, I would say that 'thing' is the den of the white bear." Charles replied.

The oddly shaped den was thin at the top, wide at the bottom, and a colorful cloud of green, blue, yellow and purple rose from an opening at the top. The bears quietly observed.

Charles positioned himself in front of them to view the structure. "Now, I have been told something that is considered quite important. We are to wait outside until we are invited in or the bear addresses us."

"Why?" asked Mato.

"Some sort of custom and we don't want to appear rude. They say this bear knows magic." Charles responded.

"Magic?" Ursula asked.

"Yes, magic. It is the sort of thing that happens, but there is no way to logically explain it, understand how, or even why it happens." Charles said.

"Like aurora borealis coming out of his den?" Ursula asked.

"Ah, yes," replied Charles, "like the northern lights colors rising from his den."

"Is magic melting the ice?" Mato wondered aloud.

"That is a very good question, Mato," Nana joined in the conversation. "It is one of many questions that I would like to ask this white bear. I understand that he is a wise bear from another land, with fur of our color, but a body not of our shape. He is a keeper of the old ways, like us, and comes from a great bear heritage."

"Like us!" exclaimed Ursula.

"I think Nana is saying, we're the same—but different," Mato said.

"Something like that," Nana nodded. "Everyone, it is time to rest. This has been an eventful day, to say the least. We have to conserve our energy. Yesterday's meal will not last us much longer and soon we must hunt again. That may require another long trek with our next meal uncertain…"

As soon as Nana had said, "Time to rest," Mato and Ursula plopped down back to back. Before Nana had finished talking, Mato had started to snore.

CHAPTER FIVE

THE HUMANS

Charles waited and watched Nana as she cuddled close to her grown cubs. She let out a long sigh. Charles knew that she wouldn't have much longer with her children. They would soon be on their own. He thought about how he would also miss Nana.

Mato stirred, "Nana?" he asked softly.

"Yes, Mato"

"Thank you for teaching us all a mother should."

"You are welcome, my grown son."

"Nana?"

"Yes, Mato."

"Will you teach me more? More than a mother should?"

"What is it, Mato?"

"Tell me about the humans…did you ever see one?" Mato persisted.

Nana sat up. Both cubs turned and looked at her. A tear rolled down Nana's cheek. "I didn't want to tell this story, but I see now that I must. It is now something that a mother must teach."

Charles also sat up a few feet away, staring intently at Nana. All listened closely to Nana's story.

"I saw humans once, and vowed to never again set my eyes upon them. I was with my brother." Mato and Ursula looked at each other then back to Nana. "We cubs were half your age, but our Nana had already taught us many, many things about survival, as I have taught you." Nana stared off for a moment, "We were so small next to her…" She looked back at the others. "Our Nana had told us about two-leggeds—the humans—she called them two-leggeds. She said that if we ever saw them to run as fast as we could and get as far away as possible. She said to act the same as if a large hungry male had caught our scent. She said that if we saw any of the humans' machines—in the air or on the sea—to run as fast and far as we could. A human machine could be anything that wasn't bird, animal, or fish."

"One day, we followed the coastline to the nearest seal harbor to hunt. Our Nana spotted a machine on the water. It was still, embedded in the coastline. She told us to run inland, so we did. We heard a noise ahead of us. There were four-leggeds that looked like big foxes, all tied together and yelling."

"Dogs," interjected Mato.

Nana glared at him. Mato sunk down and whispered, "The Churchill bears told me about them."

Nana continued, "The, ahem, *dogs* were pulling a machine with the two-leggeds on it. We ran right past them! The two-leggeds hollered and started chasing us! Our Nana ran right beside us, telling us to run faster and faster to the ice bluffs where we could hide. I ran as fast as I could, I even closed my eyes." Tears were streaming down Nana's face.

"Oh, Nana!" whimpered Ursula.

Nana raised her paw, and looked away, "That is when it happened. We heard a loud noise, like a big ice sheet cracking. My brother and I kept running until we reached the ice bluffs.

We realized Nana wasn't with us. We turned to look back, quickly hid, and then peeked out. We could smell our Nana, like never before. She was still yelling, 'Run, children, run! *Run my cubs!*' Then *crack*—we heard the noise again. Our Nana was silent."

Mato and Ursula wiggled with discomfort. Mato stared in disbelief, "She fell, right?" Ursula whimpered into his shoulder, her head turned away from her mother.

"No, and please don't interrupt." Nana sniffed. "We could see our Nana lying in the snow, not very far away, with red, like at the hunt. The two-leggeds walked over to her with a stick and *crack,* again. We saw fire come out of the stick. The two-leggeds had hunted down our Nana. My brother and I couldn't move. We could only watch as one of them called to the four-leggeds. Both two- leggeds struggled to lift our dear Nana onto their machine."

They sat still for a moment. Ursula quietly sobbed. Mato was dumbfounded.

"This is why I have taught you certain things, and kept you far away from any two—I mean, *humans.* In your new and precious life, I have been able to keep you from them. You and the four litters before you. All of you have thrived. But now I have no choice but to tell you about humans." Nana wiped her face.

"Permission to speak, Nana?" Mato asked softly while raising his paw.

"Yes, Mato."

"What did you do? What did you and your brother do?"

"We survived," Nana said plainly. "We relied on what our Nana taught us and each other until we were grown. As a grown cub, I vowed never to encounter another human. My brother…" Nana drifted off. She cleared her throat and wiped her face again. With a stern expression, she continued, "My brother made a very different vow that decided his fate." The cubs stiffened as their mother became angry. Noticing this, Nana cleared her throat again and sighed. "That is all I have to say right now."

Charles stood up and walked over to Nana. "I will let Charles tell you what we know of my brother. I need to rest now."

She strolled away a few feet. She curled up into a deep slumber. Each cub quietly walked over to Nana and nuzzled her. They went back to Charles who was sitting upright and ready to tell them the rest of the tale.

CHAPTER SIX

INVITATION

Charles delighted in storytelling mode, even when the recollection was difficult and emotional. He enjoyed talking to the cubs. He was proud to assist in teaching them. "Nana's brother was also a legendary, mighty hunter. As two young cubs, they had to do everything themselves. Searching and scenting, hunting and navigating. Nana just assumed that her brother, like herself, would never want to see a human again. They never discussed what happened that fateful day. So she did not know that in her brother's heart a deadly anger grew—and made him want revenge."

"Revenge?" asked Mato.

"Something Nana hopes you will never want, ever! Revenge is a desire to punish someone who you feel has wronged you, and it can take over a bear. He sought this against the hunter that killed his own mother—"

"Oh, *no*! I see where this is going—" Ursula exclaimed.

"Shhh," Mato put his paw over her mouth, "Nana is sleeping."

"Ahem," Ursula whispered in her fake British accent, "Pardon me."

"May I please continue without interruption?" Charles scoffed. The cubs nodded. "When Nana and her brother were grown, they went their separate ways. She never saw him again, but word got back to her that he was taken by humans."

"Taken? Not killed? Like taken to bear jail?" Mato asked.

"Bear jail?" Ursula questioned.

"Yeah, like the one in Churchill," Mato explained.

"Something similar I think, but it has an odd name." Charles thought for a moment then said, "I believe it is zoo."

"Zoo?" Mato and Ursula looked at each other.

"May I *please* finish?" Charles continued. "Nana's brother was determined to hunt down and kill the humans. He did not intend to drag them away, like his Nana was. He wanted to tear them apart, leaving their parts behind for the scavenger birds because their flesh and was not worthy of a meal. As soon as he parted from your Nana, he went back to the place where their mother was killed. He stalked and hunted a human den. There were more machines, including ones that flew and others that moved like the dog machine without dogs to pull it. He hunted the first two-legged he saw. Right away, a human with a crack stick hit him from behind. But, this crack stick did not kill. Nana's brother became very still, but not asleep. He could not move, but he was aware, as the humans took him away."

"To a zoo." Ursula commented.

"Correct, my dear, a zoo." Charles agreed.

"Wait, you just described what happens in Churchill—what exactly is a zoo?" Mato asked.

"A zoo is a place where they keep all kinds of creatures for the humans to look at."

"Like bear jail?" Mato asked.

"Is it cold?" Ursula questioned.

"Sort of, Mato. And I don't know, Ursula. I have never been to one, but I've heard that it is very boring. Creatures are confined to very small spaces and they just sit there. There is no hunting and no survival skills. They are handed nourishment prepared by humans and have no freedom."

"Doesn't sound all that bad—" Mato started.

"Are you crazy?" Ursula admonished.

"Shhh," Charles quieted them and nodded toward Nana. She had lifted her head and was looking over at the white bear den. The den was a triangle shaped structure narrow at the top and wider at the bottom, near the ice, with a hole in the pointed top. It looked like an upside-down cone.

They could see an odd-shaped white bear standing outside the den and holding a wooden staff with feathers hanging from it. He completely ignored Charles and the cubs and directed his attention toward Nana.

"I have been expecting you, wise and powerful grandmother. Come, sit with me around the ancestors, and let us talk about the strange happenings around us all." He pointed toward the den opening and made a sweeping motion with his staff, the feathers dangled.

Nana smiled and ambled right into the den without looking around, sniffing, or pausing before the white bear. He followed behind her. Charles and the cubs simply watched in awe.

The three of them watched and listened. It seemed that Nana had been in the white bear's den for hours. Occasionally, the colorful cloud would rise out of the den opening swirling with colors, blue, green, indigo, and sometimes orange.

"What are they doing?" asked Ursula.

"How long are they going to stay in there?" Mato asked.

"I do not know, grown ones. I do not know." Charles responded.

Charles jumped, "Look, Nana's paw!" Nana was waving for the others to enter the den.

Mato and Ursula approached slowly, cautiously sniffing and surveying. Once the cubs were inside, Ursula peeked out of the opening, "C'mon, Charles!" The fox pranced into the den proudly.

Inside the den was a hole dug from the snow and filled with large, round chunks of clear ice that then glowed with the same colors as the clouds that rose from the den.

Ribbons decorated the walls to mark each directional space around the circular den. The white bear sat next to the opening in the east, marked with a yellow ribbon. Nana was beside him to the north, which was marked with a white ribbon. Mato sat in the west with its black ribbon, and Ursula rested to the south, near a red ribbon. Charles seated himself in the southeast. All sat silently. Mato and Ursula stifled their many questions and anxiously waited for the white bear to speak.

CHAPTER SEVEN

SPIRIT BEAR

The white bear spoke. "My name is *Wanbli Mato Ska Wichasha Wakhan Wamakhashkan. Emakiyapi Roland.*" He looked around at their blank stares and resorted to English. "My name is Eagle White Bear Holy Man Living Being of the Earth. They call me Roland, and so may you. I am a Spirit Bear from a place called Refuge. The two-leggeds took our land with their machines. I am the last of my kind. I have been guided by the Great Spirit to come here to this barren ice and snow land. It is my heart's desire to deliver a message to you—the other white bear, the North Bear, the polar bear. Nanuqa and I have discussed the sea that is now too vast for a return to the tundra. The ice is changing and North Bears are acting strange, many feeding from the waste of the two-leggeds."

As Roland spoke, he gestured with his front paws, in sweeping motions. "Black gold drives the two-leggeds mad. Long ago, two-leggeds ravaged my homeland for the standing people, the trees. Other two-leggeds made a law to stop it and save our land for generations to come. But when they thirsted for the black gold, no law could keep them away. The black gold is the fuel for their machines. They will always hunger for it and never be full. Two-leggeds know only how to take from our Mother Earth and give no thanks for her bounty.

"I have invited you here to give you a message, in honor of all our relations. All of the four-leggeds, the winged ones, the standing trees, the stone ancestors, the fishes and the crawly things, and, yes, even the two-leggeds, for they are all our relations and we ask Great Spirit to remind us we are One. We ask the Great Spirit to touch our hearts with our prayers to remember that the Earth is our mother and we are here to honor her precious gifts for sustenance, and not for mere consumption. May we all be happy with what sustains us and find the joy of sharing with each other. Our lands may be taken and our ice may be melting, but the old ways have endured."

Roland paused for a moment, and then motioned to the colored chunks of ice, "Let us honor our ancestors, in a good way. Let us ask for new ways to honor Mother Earth and leave her replenished. Even you, solitary North Bears, will come together to get the most of your sustenance and for the survival of your tribe. Let this be an example to the two-leggeds."

He paused again and seemed to be reflecting on the stones in front of them. Mato shifted anxiously. Roland looked at him, "You, Mato, are the son of bears. Bear is your name. You are here to lead bears to their sustenance, which may be done only by working together. You will find a great ally in a bear who has come before you and who knows your Nana well. He will help you in your quest for the white whale and the unicorn whale."

Mato looked at Roland, puzzled.

Roland turned his attention to Ursula, "You, Ursula, are a princess warrior. You are the last of the bear princesses to be born unto the great Nanuqa. Like your mother before you, you possess the power of all the grandmothers of the seven generations before you and the seven generations to come. A leader you will be, not only to your cubs, but as a welcome guide to many female bears on their journeys."

Ursula looked at Nana, who nodded in agreement. Ursula blushed.

Roland looked over at Charles. "You, Charles, are truly a shifty one. You are hiding great power within your small body. Ahh, but you use such power in a good and noble way. You carry the message of support from the Great Spirit. You have assisted—and will continue to assist—many with their visions."

Charles bowed his head to Roland, then sat as straight as he could.

Roland turned to Nana, and they smiled at each other. They each put a paw over their hearts. He reached behind his back and pulled out a round drum and a small stick. He hit the stick against the drum. He played it like the beat of a heart. He passed the drum to Nana, who continued the heartbeat rhythm.

He then raised his arms up and shouted, "I call on the Great Spirit, Mother Earth, and the powers of the north, the south, the east, and the west. I call upon the four-leggeds, the winged ones, the fishes, the crawling creatures, and the standing trees. And, yes, I call upon the two-leggeds to join us in this circle—the circle of a beating heart, the circle of healing and direction."

As he shouted, the ice stones glowed with luminescent colors, unlike flames, more like northern lights. Mato looked at Ursula and nodded toward the ice stones, and she nodded back, acknowledging what they were seeing.

Roland lowered his arms and Nana stopped drumming. "Aho," said Roland, waving the strange colors toward him. "Our ancestors are here with us now."

Mato tried to be very subtle about looking around for new guests.

Roland continued, "We must honor these ancient ones and all our relations, for they are the power of our hearts."

He pulled out a pouch from behind his back and sprinkled something over the ice stones that made them sparkle like stars. "We honor the Star Nation as well, where some of us shall soon reside." He waved his hands to send the luminous colors all around them. "Let us feel the power of the Great Creator within us, healing our hearts, and knowing that, as we are healed, others are healed. We are given direction to follow our hearts, each to find his or her own True North, and honor—in a good way— our time here on Mother Earth."

Nana drummed again for several beats, then ended with two loud ones.

"Let us now rest here, in the quiet knowing of our hearts." Roland nodded to each, and then leaned to one side and curled up to rest.

Mato and Ursula looked to Nana, who nodded to each, and then she curled up. Mato and Ursula stared wide-eyed at each other. Charles stood up, turned around twice, and then lay down and curled up as well. Ursula shrugged at Mato, lay on her side with her head propped on her elbow, and watched the colorful chunks of ice. Mato reluctantly lay on his back, crossed his paws over his chest, and watched the colors escape from the hole at the top of the den.

While Nana, Roland, and Charles rested, Mato and Ursula shifted and fidgeted. Both were wide-awake. They had no idea what the strange bear was talking about. How did he make the ice chunks glow? Who does a polar bear lead? What did any of this have to do with finding good hunting? How did Nana know this bear? There were so many questions, and the answers from this bear just made more questions. A loud snore from Roland startled them and seemed to wake him.

Roland sat up and waited for the others to do the same.

CHAPTER EIGHT

OLD FRIENDS AND NEW STARS

Mato and Ursula watched Nana closely. They waited for her to rise before they did the same.

Ursula raised a front paw, "May I ask a question?"

"Aho," grunted Roland.

Ursula looked to Nana, who nodded her head.

"Mr. Roland, how do you know our mother? You two seem like old friends." She bowed her head shyly. Roland looked to Nana and she nodded toward him.

"Ah, with the great Nanuqa's permission," Roland began, "I will tell you how I came to know the one you call Nana."

Mato, Ursula, and Charles sat up straight and listened intently. Nana nodded for him to proceed.

"As I have told you, I am a Spirit Bear from the land called Refuge. It is in parts known as Alaska and Canada. The two-leggeds, the humans, drove us from our homeland. I am the last of my kind. I only survive because of the generosity and kindness of the great Nanuqa, and, of course," he pointed upward, "Wakan Tanka, the Great Spirit. When I arrived in the northland tundra, I did not know what to eat. I did not know how to hunt. These things I knew at Refuge, but I could find no salmon—fish—on the cold barren land of ice and snow. I was very young—about your age—yet determined to share the message of the Spirit Bear. Your Nana came upon me—ready to tear me apart as if I were a male polar bear intruder. I spoke to her in my native language, honoring her warrior spirit. She softened as she moved in closer to me, and I sat humbly as she sniffed. She realized I meant no harm to her, and began to walk away. I knew in my heart that she was a great warrior and would lead me to sustenance, so I followed her. She didn't seem to mind the company and she willingly shared what she had hunted with me. For an entire moon, we walked the tundra and ice floes together, and learned how to communicate, but mostly in quiet. She taught me how to hunt in your Northland and I taught her about True North and the ways of the Great Spirit."

Roland sat quietly for a moment, and then chuckled, "You might even say I was her first cub!" He and Nana laughed out loud.

Mato and Ursula looked at each other open-mouthed. They closed them quickly as Nana proceeded to speak. "I was still very young myself and I had just parted from my brother, who I traveled with after our mother was killed by the humans. I was happy for a friend. It relieved my sadness and fear of being alone. I am grateful for this Spirit Bear who taught me about True North. I am also grateful to be here now, that he has made the journey even farther to the ice cap to talk about True North to you now." She began to drum again. She and Roland sang:

> Wazei *(Wah-ZEE-eye)* Oh oh Wazei
> Wazei Oh oh Wazei
> Hi Oh Wazei
> Hi Oh Wazei
> Oh Hey Oh Hey Oh Hey Oh Heeey

They repeated it four times. Nana ended with two strong drumbeats.

Roland explained, "The Wazei are the Great Giants of the North." He pointed over Nana toward the north ribbon of white. He looked to Mato and Ursula, "You may call upon these Spirit Beings for strength and direction."

Charles cleared his throat, and Nana and Roland nodded to him, "I would like to inquire further about True North. As I understand from what you said previously, it means to follow one's heart. Am I correct in thinking so?"

Nana looked at Roland who nodded for her to answer. "True North is the result of our discernment between what we think we should do and what we know to do. I might think I should head in one direction to find my dinner, but I may *know* that I need to head in another direction. In *knowing* I am connected to the Great Spirit and I must trust that quiet, still voice—more like a feeling—instead of what I think I am supposed to do. Do you understand?"

"Yes, yes," Charles said excitedly, "I've observed you many times. You often pause and become quiet before proceeding toward the hunt. I certainly don't have the nose of a polar bear, and I have questioned your decisions at times—mostly when I first knew you—but you always found the hunt. I came to trust this, this, instinct of yours—"

"True North!" Ursula blurted out. She covered her mouth almost as soon as she said it.

"Aho," Nana and Roland confirmed in unison.

Mato shook his head, as if he had water stuck in his ears. Ursula dropped her paw and looked at Mato with concern.

Roland spoke to Ursula, "Do not be concerned about your brother, warrior princess. He may not understand here," he pointed to his head, "but he has knowing here," he pointed to his heart. "He naturally follows True North."

45

Mato sighed. He then shrugged, "I always have been a doer."

Nana reminded him softly, "A little pause before the doing may be necessary from time to time."

"Yes, ma'am," Mato blushed and looked at Charles.

"Aho," said Roland, "It is time for you to go, to take all that you have learned and choose your path in a good way. You can follow the scents, the stars, the ice, the winds, or each other. But always follow your heart and heed the quiet voice within you."

He turned and rose to all fours, bowed his head to the ground, muttered something in his strange language, and exited the den. Nana followed, also bowing her head to the ground as she left the den. Mato, Ursula, and Charles then followed. Each animal circled clockwise around the ice chunks and out the den's opening.

Roland retrieved his feathered staff and stood outside of the den. He put his left front paw over his heart and nodded to each of them. He looked at Charles and they bowed to each other.

"Well, grown ones," started Charles, "Shall we?" He began to walk away from the den. Mato and Ursula looked at each other and shrugged. They followed Charles. After a few paces, Mato and Ursula stopped and looked back at the den. Nana and Roland stood, leaning against one another.

Ursula asked, "Nana, aren't you coming?"

Nana gave her daughter a final loving stare. Then she and Roland turned and retreated into the den. Ursula let out a soft cry, and looked at Mato. He held out a paw to Ursula and she rushed to him, burying her nose into his chest. Mato sniffled as he embraced his sister. They silently began to follow Charles, who kept clearing his throat. All three listened to the heartbeat drum sound coming from the Spirit Bear den.

They reached a nearby ridge and took one last look at the den. The colorful lights streamed into the bright blue sky. Mato reached for Ursula, "Yeah, bro, I see it too," she said. They sat down to watch the colors fill the sky.

Charles broke the silence, "Oh my, could it be?"

Awestruck, the bears answered, "Uh huh…"

They saw the bright white forms of Nana and Spirit Bear dancing in the brightly colored lights. Then the white forms swirled into the colors, twisting upward into the sky. They raised their heads to watch as the swirl moved directly overhead. Charles and the bears blinked in reaction to a flash as bright as the sun. Upon opening their eyes, they saw two bright stars glowing against the blue sky.

Charles trotted closer to the bears, "I believe this is what Sir Roland meant by the Star Nation."

Mato and Ursula fell onto their backs and stared at the two stars. Mato turned to his sister, "I guess she really will always be watching over us."

"Yeah," replied Ursula, "always showing us the way to True North."

A tiny squeaky, sniffling sound pulled them from their ponderings. Ursula rolled onto her paws quickly, "Really, Charlie, I—"

Charles jumped. "Ahem!" he cleared his throat as he kept his distance from Ursula, trying to overcome his tears. "Well, there you have it…Star Nation, ahem! Shall we move onward then?"

Mato sat up and looked up at the star one more time. "We shall, dear Charles."

Mato looked at Ursula who smiled at him and said, "We shall."

"Ahem, well carry on then." Charles led the way.

CHAPTER NINE

CHOICE POINT

After a few hours, Mato was leading the way with Ursula directly behind. Charles trailed a few paces back.

Mato wondered about what the Spirit Bear had told them about themselves. He understood the True North part, but he wondered about the bear he was going to meet and hunting the white whale. He had no concept of what a unicorn whale might be. He had heard of a whale, but certainly not a unicorn one. It sounded made-up. Maybe it was some sort of magic again. Maybe he would discuss it with the others.

Ursula stopped, "Hold up, Mato, I think we should go this way," she pointed to their right.

Mato stopped reluctantly, wanting to continue forward, "No," he insisted, "it's this way."

Ursula methodically sniffed the air in each direction. She paused and turned back to Mato, pointing again to their right, "My heart tells me this way," she urged.

Mato bowed his head and shook it. He turned toward the right where Ursula pointed, stood for a moment, then turned back toward the direction he was already headed. He sat down, now sounding a bit confused, he said, "But my heart tells me this way."

By this time, Charles had caught up to them. "Is this a rest stop?" he asked panting. Ursula and Mato looked at him.

"More like a crossroads," said Ursula.

Mato explained, "Ursula wants to turn right and head that way, but I want to keep moving forward this way."

"I see," said Charles, "and this is what your heart is telling each of you?" Mato and Ursula nodded. Charles sat quietly, happy for a few moments to rest while the bears realized their dilemma.

Ursula sat down next to Mato. They crossed their arms and each looked in the direction they wanted to go. Then slowly, they began to turn toward each other. When they met each other's gaze, they jumped up and embraced.

Ursula quickly moved Mato into a headlock and rubbed his head with her other front paw, "One more for the road, big brother?"

Mato broke free and puffed himself up onto two legs, towering over his sister. Then he dropped to all fours and sadly commented, "I'm going to miss you, sis."

"Yeah, me too," she replied gently as she pushed against his shoulder.

Mato looked over at Charles, "What does this mean for you, Charles?"

"As a true gentleman, it is my desire to accompany the lady," Charles replied.

Mato turned his full body toward Charles, and stood a few feet away on two legs. He held one front paw behind him, moved the other across his belly, and bowed so low that his face was at the same level as Charles's face. He lifted his head slightly to look at the fox, "Sir Charles, it has been my pleasure."

Mato bowed his head back down, staying in this low position until Charles responded, "Oh, no, Master Mato, the honor has been mine."

Mato looked up to see the fox's tiny bow, and then stood on all fours again. "But before we go," Mato started, "do either of you know what a unicorn whale is?" Charles and Ursula laughed. Mato figured that was a no.

As the laughter subsided, all three looked up at the sky to see two stars twinkling overhead. They looked at each other and smiled one last time. Mato continued to walk forward and Ursula turned to the right, with Charles a few paces behind her.

Mato wandered onward awhile. He knew he was going back to the ocean where he had met the other male bears. He was getting hungry and needed to hunt. Yet he was feeling listless, and not in a hurry to arrive at his next destination. More had happened in the past few days than in his entire life and he felt heavier than his own massive weight. He eventually plopped down onto the cool snow, slid on his belly with his front paws at his side, and pushed along with his back paws. This was his favorite way to cool down on the ice. All the walking and parting of the ways had him overheated. When he felt sufficiently cooled, he rolled over onto his back and looked up into the sky. There he saw the stars again, and smiled. He was amazed at how bright they were in full daylight. There was mostly light this time of year, as spring began to turn into summer. He wondered if he'd come across a white whale like the one the Spirit Bear spoke of anytime soon. He started to think about the ice coast again and felt an urge to go swimming. He loved to swim, and had not done so since his last race with Ursula. "I won," he murmured to himself. Already missing his sister, he wistfully thought of her. Suddenly, an object entered his view of the sky.

It was a tiny object at first, but grew larger. Then he heard a strange noise. "Whirlybird," he said aloud to himself. He scrambled onto his feet. "That must be one of those whirlybirds the males were talking about!" He became excited and moved toward it, but then remembered the concerns about humans. He decided to stay where he was and observe.

As the black object moved closer, Mato saw something hanging below it. The helicopter came into full view and Mato clearly saw a white object dangling beneath it. Mato watched as the human machine hovered in the sky, slowly moved closer to the ground, and gently placed the white object on the ground.

"A bear!" Mato shouted, then covered his mouth. Feeling both silly that no one could hear him, but also nervous that the humans would notice. He watched closely as a cable was released and the whirlybird lowered to the ground near the bear. Mato was amazed by the way the machine stirred up the snow on the ice pack, like a sudden storm. He saw two humans move out from the cloud of snow and hurry toward the bear. They removed a blanket from the bear and hustled back to the machine. The whirlybird moved into the sky again, leaving a small windstorm and the bear below.

When Mato could no longer hear or see the human machine, he trotted over to the bear.

CHAPTER TEN

SPECIAL DELIVERY

Mato moved quickly yet cautiously, pausing often to sniff the air and the ground. Definitely a polar bear, he wondered if this bear came from the "bear jail" that the male bears had talked about. Mato slowly approached the motionless bear, walking in a slow circle around it. He could tell that the bear was male, about his height, but thinner. He noticed an odd odor—like that of Slick's—that was fading. The bear had a strange green tint to his fur like the color of kelp. Mato and Ursula used to chew the kelp they found along the Canadian shoreline while waiting for the sea water to freeze.

Mato continued walking around the bear, narrowing the circle until he could hear the bear breathing. The bear continued to lie there with his mouth and eyes open. Even his breathing seemed motionless. Mato sat beside the bear and watched him breathe for several minutes.

Finally, the bear opened and closed his mouth. He sniffed loudly, but lay still, unable to lift his head. He was fully aware of Mato's presence. Mato jumped to all fours as the bear said matter-of-factly, "I'm not good eatin', if that's what you're after."

Mato stood where the bear could see him, "I'd rather not eat my own kind." Mato returned to his comfortable seat beside the motionless bear.

The bear chuckled, "Yeah, well, I'm obviously no match for you, even as young as you are. But I bet I could teach you a thing or two, and I can certainly use your help."

Mato sighed, "How do you guys always know I'm young? What kind of help? Do you need me to carry you somewhere?"

The bear chuckled again, "An older bear might not be so curious. And, no, you do not need to carry me. I should be up and moving in a few minutes. But, I haven't been way out here in a long time, and I'll need help adjusting again—I haven't hunted since I was your age."

Mato slid closer to the bear, then slid onto his belly and propped his head up on his paws. He sprawled out with his elbows planted in the snow. Mato figured he'd get comfortable while they chatted. "Why can't you move? Did the humans hit you with a fire stick?"

"Something like that," the bear replied, now lifting his head, but letting it drop back down. "It's called a tranquilizer and it takes a while to wear off. I sure do appreciate the company."

Mato nodded, unwilling to admit to the bear that he was feeling a bit lonely himself. So many questions went through Mato's mind. How could this bear seem healthy yet so thin? Mato knew a bear's thickness was essential to survival. How would this bear survive the Arctic ice cap in winter with all the storms and subzero temperatures? And what was that thing on his ear? Mato shifted, trying to hide his curiosity.

The bear twitched his paws a little, "Go ahead, kid, ask me anything. I know you're young. I can answer all those male bear questions that your momma never told you."

Mato jolted upright. How did this bear know his Nana did not tell him things? "Now that you mention it, I've learned more in the past few days from my—about my—well, I can say I've learned more since my last meal than in my entire life!"

The bear chuckled again, this time lifting his head and stretching all four paws out straight, "Life is like that, kid. One minute, you are in your mother's care and the next minute you are on your own."

Mato plopped back down, "Tell me about it, I had a sister, too." He sat next to the bear watching him try to move each part. "Seriously," Mato implored, "tell me about it."

The bear slowly moved himself into a seated position as he spoke, "Tell you about life?" He stretched his front paws from this seated position, "Well, most recently I have been a part of an experiment. I have been removed from the care of humans and returned to the wild, as they call it." He started to feel around his neck for something, "I'm sure they've attached something to track me."

"I think it's on your ear," Mato pointed.

The bear felt the thing on his ear, "Yep, they're gonna keep an eye on me." He confirmed. The bear tugged at his ear then shook his head as he prepared to move onto all fours, "This is how the humans can keep track of me. It's called a tag. They want to know how long—and even if—I can survive in my natural habitat after being in captivity for so long."

"Is captivity like bear jail?" Mato asked.

"Captivity is a zoo, I don't know what bear jail is." The bear replied.

Mato's eyes widened, "Please tell me more about the zoo—I'll try to explain bear jail later, I'm not too sure myself."

"Sure, kid," the bear stood on all fours and rocked side to side trying to shake off the effects of the tranquilizer. "A zoo is a place where a bunch of humans keep all sorts of animals for other humans to look at."

Mato tilted his head, "Did you like the zoo?"

"Yes and no," the bear replied as he attempted to stand on two legs, "I was angry, at first. But they fed me, though the food took getting used to. And I could just play all the time. But it was also hot and really boring because I didn't get to leave the small area they put me in."

"They fed you?" Mato asked incredulously.

"Yeah," said the bear, dropping to all fours. "After a while, I got used to the fishiness of the food, and I didn't need to eat as much because I wasn't doing anything—no walking or swimming long distances, no hunting, and I didn't have to use energy to keep warm. It was more difficult to stay cool. As you can see, there isn't much blubber left on me, so I don't have a lot of insulation. Even so, I would paddle around in circles in the small pool they had for me just to be in the water."

"Pool?" Mato asked, again noticing how thin this bear was.

"Yeah, pool. Like a small hole in the ice, but not very deep. Not deep at all. All I did was entertain the humans who came to look at me. Most days I didn't feel like moving at all, it was too hot. But, occasionally, I would get into the pool water, go under, and flip around or play with a toy. The humans loved that. They could see me through glass under the water."

Mato kept listening, not fully understanding, but mesmerized by the story.

"The worst part was it *never* snowed there—not once! Sometimes, when it was crazy hot, they used this machine that makes wind, called a fan, and put ice in front of it. I could sit in that mist all day." The bear was now walking around a bit, he stretched his arms up and stood up on his two hind legs. "Well, kid, I need to get moving, I'm cold and hungry."

"Yeah," Mato agreed, "I'm hungry too. Would you like to hunt with me? You said you needed help."

"Great!" said the bear, "but just to clarify, your mom did teach you to be solitary? I assume this was supposed to be your first solitary hunt."

Mato nodded his head up and down, "She taught me well, and I had to feed myself during the last while with her. She made my sister and I get our own meals. She left her scraps for other animals before sharing with us. Besides, I usually have some to share and I know you are in no condition to challenge me."

"You got that right," said the bear with a shiver, "By the way, we haven't been properly introduced yet- my zoo name is Umky." He held out his front paw.

"Pleasure to meet you," Mato replied, shaking Umky's paw with his. "My name is Mato."

Umky froze, still holding Mato's paw. He became paler than white, even the green tint seemed to vanish.

Mato slowly released his paw, "What happened? Did the tranquilizer come back?"

Umky shivered, "Umky is the name the zoo humans gave me—my real name is also Mato."

The bears stared at each other without moving.

NAMESAKE

"Wait, what?" Mato was confused. "Your name is Umky, but your name is also Mato, like mine?"

Umky nodded then asked, "Who gave you that name?"

Mato looked at him with a strange glance, "My mother, of course."

Umky became impatient, "I know your mother gave it to you, I guess I should ask, who is your mother?"

"Nana," Mato said plainly.

"That's it?" Umky pressed him, "Just plain old Nana? Is that short for something?"

Mato sighed loudly then waved his front paws up, "Nana, short for Nanuqa, the great Nanuqa, known as the mighty huntress—sheesh—*everyone* knows my mother."

Umky began to sniff about wildly, "You just left her didn't you? Is she near? Can I see her?"

Mato became concerned with Umky's agitation; "No, she's— she is..." Mato could not bring himself to say she was dead, so he moved slowly over to Umky, who stood still for a moment.

Mato put one paw on Umky's shoulder and pointed with the other to the star in the sky, "She is there."

Umky looked upward, saw the two stars, and one twinkled. He looked at Mato, who nodded, then looked up again. Suddenly, the zoo bear fell to his knees, sobbing.

Mato did not know what to do. Sure, he had seen a sniffle or two from a bear. Even his sister shed a tear when his mother left, but this? He waited to ask this zoo bear how he knew his mother. Mato thought to himself, we have the same name. Could this be the bear in the story that Charles told about Nana, her mother, and brother? Could this be the bear that the Spirit Bear spoke of? Mato slowly kneeled down on his hind legs and gently moved Umky's paws away from his face and looked at him, "Are you my uncle?"

The bear nodded his head, rubbed his snout, and returned Mato's gaze, "Yes, it seems that I am. Nanuqa is…was my sister."

Mato and Umky could do nothing else but hug one another. They did not hug as though they would begin to wrestle; they relaxed into each other and savored the moment of knowing that they were no longer alone. Umky began to shiver again, so he and Mato released their embrace and started walking, side by side and conversing like old friends.

Mato asked, "Do you want me to call you Uncle Mato?"

Umky replied, "That sounds real nice, but no. I haven't been called Mato in years and, besides, I'm used to Umky now. I think it's Siberian or something."

Mato asked, "Is Mato a Canadian name? I mean, since we're from Canada?"

Umky chuckled, "Actually, I think our name came from somewhere else—I remember my mother told me it means bear in some language. Not polar bear, but just bear. I guess there are brown and black bears too. Umky actually means polar bear for some humans in Siberia. It's complicated. Humans are complicated."

"Do you remember a lot about your mother?"

"Heck ya," snorted Umky, "And about your mother too!"

Mato bowed his head for a moment, "Please tell me about them Uncle—Uncle Umky!"

"Nice, kid, that has a wonderful ring to it…Uncle Umky… In a lot of ways, I am a better bear as Umky. It is very rare that a male polar bear encounters his own kin. So, you tell me first, kid, how much of my story do you know?"

Mato snorted, "Not much! Our fox friend, Charles, just told Ursula and me the story a few days ago."

Umky stopped walking.

Mato stopped and looked back, "What now?"

Umky started walking again, "Ursula, you say?"

Mato replied, "Yeah, my sister Ursula."

"You're not gonna believe this kid, but that was our mother's name, Ursula. We called her Ursa." Umky seemed to think this was yet another amazing coincidence.

"Yeah, well, nothing surprises me anymore about our family from what I've come to know in the past week!" Mato noted.

"That's another thing, our mom Ursa used to rely on foxes for a lot of stuff, too—especially scouting info. I just thought they were annoying, and she was always telling me to be respectful. I didn't get it, respectful of a tiny little fur ball relying on our scraps?"

"That's what I said to Nana!" Mato concurred, "But I have to admit—good old Charles turned out to be handy to have around…"

"So, go on then, what did he tell you?" Umky prodded.

"This would sound so good if I could do a British accent, but I'll just give you the summary of it—"

"Let me guess," Umky interjected, "Charles was from a royal line of red foxes?"

"Pffft!" Mato nodded his head. He then relayed Charles's account of how a human killed Nana's mother, and Nana and her brother had to manage on their own. One day, they went their separate ways. Of course, they knew what happened to Nana. As for her brother, word was that the humans had captured him after he attacked one of them, so they sent him to a zoo. "How exactly did you end up at the zoo anyway?"

"Well," explained Umky, "when a bear is full of hate and anger, and seeks revenge, he does foolish things—like attack humans who don't even have enough meat on them to make a meal!"

Mato stopped walking, "Speaking of meat, I think I have a scent!" He nosed the air.

Umky copied, somewhat clumsily exclaiming, "Wow! I forgot how distinct the smell of seal can be out here! I'm used to way too many other odors interfering...but that's seal— *pure* seal!"

"OK, Uncle," Mato cautioned quietly, "refresher course?"

Umky composed himself, "Yes, please."

"First rule of hunting?" Mato whispered.

Umky made a motion with his front paw across his mouth. Mato nodded and the two proceeded forward deliberately and stealthily in the direction of the scent.

CHAPTER TWELVE

THE HUNT

Umky and Mato knew instinctively what to do—as in sniff out and track a seal—and had learned the same techniques. Mato wondered if his new partner had developed the techniques. Maybe he and Nana devised them while hunting after their mother was killed. Though Mato had been well trained to be a solitary hunter, Nana had also taught her cubs how to hunt together. Mato and Ursula learned to work as a team, one to distract and one to capture the vulnerable seal.

Umky gave Mato a knowing nod of his head, confirming his role in the hunt. Once they had the seal in their sights, Mato would be the captor, as he was the younger and swifter bear. Umky would distract the seal to give Mato a stronger advantage. Umky felt quite comfortable letting the younger bear take the lead. In fact, he was happy to have Mato there to secure his first meal. Already shivering, Umky would become quickly exhausted if he had to make solo attempts to bag his own seal.

They had come upon an ice cove where a seal on an ice sheet rested at the edge of the water. Twenty feet of water slightly separated the seal from the edge of the ice cove. So the seal lay on a twenty-five-foot ice sheet surrounded by water. This was good for the seal, as it could slip into the water from any direction and quickly escape a polar bear and certain doom. His chances were much better in the water. Though the polar bears were strong swimmers, the seal would be far too quick once fully submerged. Mato and Umky knew they had to work quickly and get to the seal before it decided to get back in the water.

Mato slipped into the sea quickly and quietly, about a hundred feet from where the seal rested on its ice sheet. He swam swiftly and stealthily, able to stay undetected and swim around to approach the seal from the ocean side.

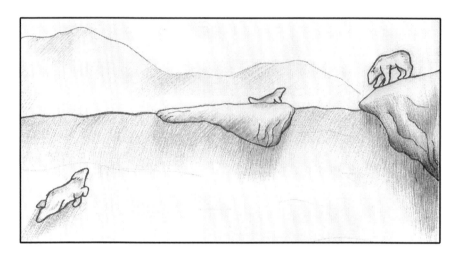

Meanwhile, Umky approached from land. He moved without making a sound across the ice, his furry paws muffling his careful footsteps. Each step was deliberate and silent. He would be getting the seal's attention, but it had to be at the precise moment when Mato was ready to spring up out of the water.

Umky moved in as close as he dared to. Umky stood on an ice sheet less than fifteen feet between the water and the ice sheet the seal lay on. Completely motionless, he kept himself hidden from the seal's view. He waited for the signal. The seal seemed to become aware of the imminent danger and turned to look in Umky's direction. Luckily, at that same moment, Umky saw an air bubble in the water on the other side of the ice sheet. He knew Mato was in position and raised his head now, getting the seal's full attention. Upon seeing Umky, the seal reacted quickly and turned to dive into the ocean only to be met by Mato bursting out of the water. Mato pinned the seal to the ice sheet and made his kill.

Umky leapt across from the main ice, barely missing the ice sheet. He ducked into the water for just a second before climbing up onto the ice sheet to witness Mato ravenously devouring the seal. Umky shook the water off from head to tail. He settled in a few feet away. Mato was the lead and Umky knew to wait his turn. Mato noticed and, without a pause from eating, grabbed a chunk of the seal blubber with his paw and tossed it to Umky.

Umky delicately gnawed at the meat, slowly chewing each mouthful and savoring every swallow. When Mato had his fill, there was still plenty left for Umky to finish. Mato was surprised that Umky had only just finished the chunk he tossed him.

Mato was curious, surely Umky needed to gain some weight, "Aren't you starving?"

Umky slowly moved over to the seal, "Of course. I just have to take it easy on this first meal. I didn't eat this rich back at the zoo."

Mato scratched the ice and pulled up some snow to his face to clear away the blood from his coat, "I thought you said they fed you?"

Umky finished chewing a mouthful, swallowed, then responded, "Yes, but they didn't feed me like this. I had to stay lean to keep cooler and keep my blubber thin—that's why I'm shivering here!" He took another bite from the seal.

Mato shrugged and, as Umky ate, slipped into the water to clean more thoroughly. He came up from the water, leaned on the ice sheet with his front paws, and watched Umky chew slowly.

Umky swallowed again, "You don't have to wait for me, I can be awhile. I have to take it slow so that I don't throw up."

Mato climbed up onto the ice sheet. "What's throw up?"

Umky paused before his next mouthful, "It's when the food you ate comes back up and out of your mouth."

Mato looked at him somewhat shocked, wondering if Umky was kidding, "Oh, OK, you just take your time." He settled in for a nap, "I'll be right here when you are ready."

Umky continued his methodical eating of the remaining seal while Mato snored.

CHAPTER THIRTEEN

ALONE AGAIN

Mato awoke to Umky cleaning himself off. Only a few scraps of the seal remained. Mato yawned and stretched while lying on his back, and rolled to his side, watching Umky clean himself meticulously. "You clean yourself as fast as you eat."

"No need to rush," said Umky while licking around the claws of one of his front paws, "Besides, cleaning aids the digestion."

"So does sleeping," Mato said, rolling onto his back again.

"No sleep for this old bear yet, now that I've stopped shivering and had a nice meal I need to move around and get myself acclimated."

Mato rolled up to a seated position, "Oh?"

"Yeah," Umky continued, "It was like I slept the whole way here from the zoo. They moved me from place to place, giving me lots of those tranquilizers. Must have been a whole week! It feels good to be able to move at all."

"OK then," Mato said rising to all four paws, "I'm ready when you are."

"Yeah, about that," Umky started, "I don't mean to be ungrateful for the fine dining and all, or seem like I don't care to have met my nephew—but, sorry to say, kid, it's time for me to go solo."

"Oh." Mato sat back down.

Umky chuckled, "Hey, kid, how about we head in further on the ice cap together?"

"You mean it?"

"Sure I do," Umky replied, as he slipped into the water to swim the few feet to shore. Mato followed. Umky climbed onto the ice shore and shook a mighty spray of water. He was just warming up and didn't want to keep any water on him.

Polar bears are essentially waterproof, so their skin doesn't get wet, but the water around their fur assists with cooling them.

Mato enjoyed the water. It was very refreshing, so he just shook his head a little as he climbed out and let the water fall from his fur, leaving a puddle trail as he walked.

"So tell me more about this fox you are friends with," Umky suggested.

"Only after you tell me how you ended up in the zoo."

"Well, remind me what the fox told you?"

"Basically, he said that you and Nana worked together until it was time for you to separate. Nana chose to stay away from humans no matter what, and you wanted to hunt them down. Then you tried to kill one and ended up in the zoo."

"That about sums it up." Umky said plainly, saying nothing more.

"C'mon, Umky, tell me about the humans and what you did that was so foolish. And what is revenge exactly?" Mato wondered to himself if Umky was the "great ally" bear that the Spirit Bear spoke of and would give him any clues about the white whale, or if he might know what a unicorn whale was.

Umky stopped and looked at Mato, "Revenge is trying to get back at someone who has wronged you," he started walking again, "I thought it was wrong that the human killed our mother, so I decided to do it back to them."

"But if you thought what they did was wrong, why did you want to do it?" Mato asked, puzzled.

Umky stopped walking, "Exactly!" He started walking, "But I thought I knew it all—that I could run them down like they did our mother. They don't pay attention very well. I spied on humans a lot, for a long time. I was careful not to get their attention. Luckily, not all humans want to hurt polar bears, but they are unpredictable. There was no pattern to what they did and didn't do. Humans aren't easy prey, like I thought.

"One day, I just got frustrated and went after one. It curled up into a ball and was hard to get a bite into—I had grabbed the outer shell, they call them coats. Before I could get a good grip I felt a pinch and then everything in my body went numb. I found myself lying next to the human. I thought I was dead, like momma, but there was no blood. Other humans ran over and the one I attacked scrambled to his feet. The others examined his coat, saw that he was OK, and then they all checked on me. There were four or five of them. I wasn't dead! I learned later that I had been knocked motionless with a tranquilizer. I could feel their concern for me. Imagine, concern after I had attacked as if it was prey! Anyway, I got sleepy and the next thing I knew I was in a whirlybird. After another tranquilizing pinch or two, I woke up in my first zoo."

Mato stopped walking. Umky stopped and watched as Mato contorted his face, shook his head, then asked, "So humans aren't bad then?"

Umky laughed, "Not really, except for the one that shot my momma. I guess humans are more like, oh, a nuisance."

"A nuisance?"

"Yeah, you know something that just kind of gets in the way of things, kind of like a fox." Umky explained.

"I've come to know the fox to be useful."

"Well, I guess you can say that about some humans." They started walking again and Umky continued, "For example, at the zoo, the humans who fed me were quite useful. But some of the ones who came to look at me were quite a nuisance! Some would yell and scream while I was napping. Some even threw stuff at me. Nuisance. I mostly liked the very young humans. You could feel their joy. It reminded me of coming out of the den that first time as a cub."

Mato daydreamed about the first time he and Ursula left the den, tumbling out into the world together, sliding on the snow, and looking up at the blue sky. He came back from his daydream, shook his head, and asked, "So, what is the best advice you can give me about humans since I don't have any experience?"

Umky said, "Well, I guess you have figured out that if one has a fire stick you should stay away, just in case it isn't a tranquilizer. Even if it is, it still isn't any fun. But, if they are holding something close to their face, something that might be square or round, not long and skinny like a fire stick, that's OK. It is a camera. I don't know what it does, but lots of humans that came to look at me had them. I was never hurt by one. The only thing they did was flash a bright light occasionally. So maybe don't look right at it because it makes your eyes spotty like after looking at the sun."

"OK, got it. Humans with fire sticks, not good. Humans with cameras, OK. In general, a nuisance."

"Ya learn fast, kid." Umky beamed.

"Well, I'd rather learn by doing, like hunting, wrestling, and swimming…but from what I've heard about humans, I think Nana made a good choice to just stay away."

"Yeah, kid, from what you told me we both had pretty smart sisters," Umky agreed.

They walked awhile without talking and Mato daydreamed about being a young cub and playing with Ursula. Mato still had many questions for Umky. He planned to follow the icy edge of the ocean to see if he could find the other males again. He figured there must be good hunting if so many males had gathered there. And now, after spending time with Umky, he felt like he knew a thing or two to impress them with. Even so, he still had lots of questions.

Umky stopped walking, "Well, kid, you gonna keep heading this way? Because I'm gonna follow the ocean edge this way." He pointed in the opposite direction of where Mato was about to turn.

Mato put his nose up in the air. They had been walking further onto the ice cap. Umky was pointing southward, while Mato was pointing to the north.

"Actually, I'm going to go this way," Mato nodded northward.

"Hee, hee," Umky chuckled, "True North—always a good direction. Well kid, I appreciate your help—maybe I'll see you or run into your sister."

For a moment, Mato forgot Umky was his uncle and he bristled. Then he realized Umky meant no harm to Ursula and decided to warn him, "Careful, Umky. Ursula is fierce. It doesn't matter that she's smaller—"

Umky raised a paw to stop Mato, "Say no more, kid, and remember *your* mother was *my* sister."

"It's your funeral," Mato chided.

"Anyway, it sounds like there may be a little fox to help with introductions," Umky replied.

Mato laughed, "Just be sure to use his proper name, Charles."

"Will do," Umky replied as he turned to be on his way.

Mato watched him walk away and wondered how Umky knew about True North. It seemed that Umky had adjusted quickly to his natural climate. He was more surefooted now and the hunt had made him thicker. His fur even looked whiter. As Mato turned to be on his own way he thought, "I have a good name."

Chapter Fourteen

THE KID IS BACK

Mato continued northward on the ice cap, the frozen island of sea ice at the North Pole—about a mile northward, toward the center—where the snowpack was easier to walk on. He nosed the air in search of the male bears gathered by the sea. When he caught a scent, he climbed over a low ridge of ice and headed back to the ice floe.

He thought about how Nana taught him everything he knew about being a solitary bear surviving in the Arctic. She taught him everything that he was supposed to do. He thought about how Ursula had constantly corrected him when he wanted to do something he wasn't supposed to. He considered the choices Umky made that got him to the zoo. And he wondered about Slick and the Churchill bears. How did females just do the right thing? He figured he could learn a lot about what *not* to do from the males.

He approached the bears cautiously, having seen the males in the same groupings as when he met them the last time. Mato walked right past Slick, who was pacing again. Slick noticed Mato and ran to him. Mato stayed on all fours, puffed himself up, and growled. Slick rose to two legs and backed up with his front paws up, "Whoa, dude, easy…" Slick dropped to all fours and paced in front of Mato, "Did you find the dump? Is it out there? Did you see the humans?"

Mato relaxed, "No, Slick, no dump—but I did see humans for a minute. They dropped off a zoo bear and left. So the bear and I hunted together—"

"What?" Slick stood up again, "You hunted with another bear? Oh, I see…" he returned to all fours, "You let him have your leftovers, like the cons do for me."

"Something like that." Mato said, walking. Slick returned to pacing.

Mato gave the wrestling Sven and Lars a wide berth as he passed. "Take that, you naughty bear!" shouted Sven.

"No. You take that more, bad bear!" Lars countered. "Ooh, I like that!"

"Hah! I got you now!" Sven persisted.

They seemed to freeze in their entwined position as Mato passed. Then they scrambled apart and stood up on their back paws.

Sven whistled and shouted, "Hey there, young man."

Lars tried to whistle, "Come and wrestle with us."

Sven added, "Ya, we give you good lesson."

Mato continued walking. Lars continued, "Ya—you need good lesson!"

Mato never turned his head to respond. Sven jumped on Lars, "That was sneaky!" Lars shouted.

"Ya, young man distract you!" Sven shouted back.

Mato really wanted to talk to Al. He seemed like the alpha bear of the group. He wondered if that was how he got his name. The three "cons" as Slick liked to call them—Al, Ket, and Oslo—were relaxing.

Oslo rolled over, "Hey, hey, look who is back. Hey kid, what do ya know?"

Ket looked up and Al stayed motionless.

Mato puffed himself up as best he could, and attempted to approach Al. Oslo jumped in front of him. "Not so fast, big baby bear." Oslo was small, but Mato could tell he'd be just a scrappy as Ursula.

Ket nosed the air, "Where you going, baby boy, without your mama?"

Mato stood his ground in front of Oslo. "Step aside, Oslo, I'd like to talk to Al." Oslo, who had no intention of challenging Mato more, stepped aside as Mato took another step forward, "Oh yeah? Well that's *Mister* Alpha to you, cub." Oslo bounced back on his hind legs and just barely shuffled out of Mato's way.

Mato continued approaching Al, who lay on his back and still had not moved. Ket huffed and hissed, but didn't move. He didn't feel like getting up.

Mato plopped down next to Al. Without moving, Al asked, "What's the matter, cub? Did Nana send you away?"

Mato completely deflated at the mention of his mother. He sat with his head bowed down and sighed. Al opened one eye to get a look at Mato.

Mato spoke quietly, "Actually, Nana is the one who went away." He looked up into the sky at the glistening star. "She's gone."

Al opened his other eye and watched the star glisten. He rolled over and stood up on all fours. Mato sat still, and kept his head down. Oslo and Ket looked at each other, and then back at Mato and Al. Al gently touched the side of Mato's muzzle with his own and whispered, "Walk with me a minute, kid." Al started walking away from Oslo and Ket, and Mato followed slowly. Al stopped for a moment so Mato was walking beside him.

Mato asked, "Aren't you supposed to pummel me or something?"

"Nah," Al replied. "I like you, kid. I liked you right away, even before I knew you were Nana's cub. Sometimes I pummel a new bear just for show. But, you see, my experience and your youth would make it a pretty even match, and I don't feel like it. Besides, we are from the same womb."

Mato gave Al a strange look, "What's a womb?" The other stuff Al had said made sense. They were the same size and about the same weight, although Mato may have been a bit heavier.

Al chuckled, "It means we have the same mother."

Mato stopped walking, "Nana is *your* mother? But, you're so—old."

"Pffft," Al snorted. "Yeah, older than you. You heard Oslo say my full name, Alpha. I didn't get that name for being the big kahuna around here. I got that name from Nana because I was her firstborn."

"Wow, that's very cool. My name just means bear." Mato tried to be humble with his newly discovered older brother.

Al lectured, "Your name means a lot more than bear. It's a heritage namesake, from our uncle."

Mato initiated walking again. "You're not gonna believe this Al, but I just spent a day with our uncle. How did you know about him?"

Mato and Al sat down and Al replied, "I saw him too, when I was young like you and on my own."

Mato stopped and bowed, "You go first with your uncle story, since you are Nana's first, Mister Alpha."

"OK, wise guy," Al took a few more steps, and sat down. Mato joined him.

"When I was just a bit younger than you, not quite the same size, Nana sent me on my own. She had taught me everything she knew, and needed to care for herself. She was still young too. I was an only cub, and I could tell it was hard for her to do what she had to. She literally chased me away. After about a half day of wandering, I smelled a male bear and a scent I didn't recognize. They were close by. I wasn't really afraid of males. I saw Nana fight a couple off when I was really young. She had taught me to stay away from them. She also warned me to stay away from humans. I had never seen one, but she told me what they looked like. Of course, I was very curious, so I had to investigate the scents. I pretended I was on a hunt so I wouldn't be noticed.

"I stayed downwind behind an ice ridge and watched a big male bear stalking something. He looked just like you do now. I know now that he was stalking a human. He just ran right after it! When the big bear pounced, the human quickly curled up, as if he were sleeping. In that same moment and without warning, I heard a loud *crack*, not like when ice cracks, but sharper and louder. Then I saw a human with a stick and two others. The bear didn't move and just lay there. The first human jumped up, and the others checked him. Then they checked the bear. I didn't know if they were going to eat him or not! A couple of the humans left and returned with a machine and a sled. They loaded that bear onto the sled and took him away."

"To the zoo," Mato added.

"Yeah, well I did not know that then. Later I learned from the fox Nana sometimes used that Uncle Mato stalked humans a lot, and that he was destined to go to a zoo—or be killed. It was in that conversation that I figured out that bear had been our uncle." Al sat quiet for a moment.

Mato explained, "That is the same story Umky just told me."

"Umky?" Al asked.

"Oh, sorry, yeah, our Uncle Mato. They gave him the name Umky at the first zoo…it also means bear, polar bear, in fact."

"Humph." Al asked, "So what is our uncle like?"

Mato said, "He's old, like you."

Al shook his head, "Did he tell you about the zoo?"

"He said it was hot and boring, but they fed him—"

Al interrupted, "They *fed* him?"

"Yeah, that's what he said." Mato continued, "After we hunted, he ate slowly. It took *forever.*"

"They *fed* him!" Al said incredulously. He stood up. "Those lousy humans never fed us bears at the compound—all we ever got was some water!"

Mato wondered what Al meant by compound. Then he thought, "Oh, he means bear jail." Mato changed the subject since he had no idea what to say about zoo, jail, or being fed by humans, "Did they have cameras?"

Al turned quickly, "What?"

"Umky, I mean, Uncle Mato said that humans had things up at their face that sometimes flashed lights," Mato explained.

"Cameras," Al repeated. "Huh, so that's what you call those things. Yeah, they all had them. Especially the ones that came to look at us in those big white machines that rolled around the tundra. The humans would peek out with those cameras. Sometimes those machines had a really good smell."

"So, Umky is right, those cameras won't pinch you and make you tranquilized?" Mato asked.

Al looked at Mato, "Tranquilized?"

"Motionless," Mato confirmed.

"Nah," Al replied, "That's what the sticks are for."

"Umky said that too, but that there are also sticks that kill you."

Al explained, "Well, I guess the humans try not to do that anymore. They seem less interested in hunting us and more curious about us. That is why they made the polar bear compound. It is a way to keep us bears away from their dens and their scrap piles. That's how the rest of us met, except for the Danes, I mean, the two bears from Greenland. Slick, of course, was right in the middle of the scrap pile. He calls it the dump.

Oslo, Ket, and me, well, we kept investigating some of the smells that we encountered around the square machines and it led us right into town! You should have seen those humans scramble! We were still a few hundred yards away when the stick carriers came and, before we knew it, we were holed up in the big tin den for three weeks! They did give us a whirlybird ride back to some nice hunting ice at least."

Mato stood up to start walking again, "I guess this is one thing I really don't want to learn by doing—dealing with humans that is. Umky and I decided that our Nana made the best choice to stay away from them."

Al stood up also, "Yeah, even when our Nana was young she was smart about that."

They started walking back to the other males. Mato thought to himself, "I think Al might be the bear who came before me, like the Spirit Bear talked about."

Chapter Fifteen

THE BIG IDEA

"You have another agenda besides a family reunion, don't ya, kid." Al said.

"In fact, I do." Mato said as he stopped walking.

"Well, let's hear it." Al stopped also.

"White whales. I want to hunt the white whale. I feel like one smaller whale could feed a half dozen bears, at least," Mato stated. Known as the beluga whale to humans, the white whale measures about nine feet and weighs over a thousand pounds.

"You'd need that many bears to do it, unless you come across one already dead," Al said.

"I know of seven bears in this vicinity alone." Mato stated proudly.

Al chuckled, "If you want to call them bears. Slick is just plain shot. He's been eating our scraps for years. Oslo and Ket are none too bright. And those other two, sure they may be clever, but they just act too damn silly to listen."

"Isn't Al short for Alpha?" Mato reminded his brother.

"OK, kid, why don't we see if they listen to you with me at your back?" Al suggested.

"So you are willing to try a whale hunt with the others?" Mato excitedly asked.

"Heck ya!" replied Al. "Our favorite meal is more difficult to find. Sure, it's easiest for us to hunt seal solo. But these days, we have to think bigger and better. One whale can keep us all going for at least a month, not to mention scraps that will feed others. But understand, little brother, it is our nature to work alone. Sure, we hang out when we are bored between hunts or when we are waiting for a freeze, and we like to kid around a lot. But come mating time, we fight hard to get with a good female. Otherwise, we go it alone. Also, we don't work well together, especially these bears here. Each has his own way of doing things."

"I get the solitary thing," Mato agreed, "and I know we won't be hanging around all the time—but, like Nana said when we couldn't swim back to the tundra because it was too far, 'These are strange times.' When we combine each bear having his own way and working together, it could result in something better."

"That's why I think you should take the lead. *You* are new. As far as these boys know, you are fresh from your momma. They don't know we're brothers." Al playfully knocked into Mato with his shoulder.

"I don't know if I should take that as a compliment or an insult. I don't know, Al. I don't think I can be as bossy as my sister." He knocked back into Al.

"Hah! I bet she kicked your butt! That is exactly what I am talking about, little brother. *No* bear has a boss. We are each the kings and queens of the Arctic. Once we are on our own, we call our own shots. As for humans, well, they are just a nuisance."

"Nuisance," Mato repeated. "That's what Umky said about humans. OK, I get it, we are solitary bears and no one is the boss of us. So tell me, Alpha, how do we get the others to come along?"

"Well, we do a little dance, put on a little show, and make them think it is all their idea."

"I'm all for the part about making them think it is their idea. Do you have any ideas for a little dance and show?"

"Of course I do. First, the show is about getting you into the fraternity. An initiation, if you will. You and I will accomplish this with a little dance where you show me some of your sister's moves." Al grinned.

"Fine. Just don't let me kick your butt too bad." Mato returned his grin.

"No worries about that, little brother, no worries."

Nonchalantly, Mato and Al returned to the area where the males gathered. The brothers were *seemingly* having a nice conversation. As they approached, the other bears noticed and turned. Slick stopped pacing.

Suddenly, Al smacked Mato's face with his front paw. Mato stopped and shook his head. Al waited for Mato to bow his head. Instead, Mato returned the slap. Al shook his head, and then turned as if walking over to Ket and Oslo. He then whirled around and pounced on Mato. The younger bear found himself on his back with Al on top of him.

The other bears gathered in closer, hollering and jeering. Al continued to hold down a wriggling Mato, turned to his audience, and let out a bellowing roar. The other bears became silent. Mato continued trying to free his front paws from under Al's grip. Trying to knock off Al, Mato kicked his back paws.

"Really, kid?" Al chided, "That's your best move?"

"No" Mato grunted, "This is!" Mato freed one front paw and swept it across under Al's chest enough to alter Al's balance and roll out from under him. As Mato stood up, Al quickly wrapped his arm around Mato's neck, and locked his front paws together under Mato's chin, holding him in a headlock. The other bears gasped at the sudden display.

"Now say 'uncle.'" Al tried to bring Mato back to the ground.

"You're no uncle," Mato said and he grabbed Al's back leg and pulled his brother to the ground with him. Al continued to hold Mato in a headlock as they both hit the snowpack.

The other bears cheered. They had never seen another bear get Al to the ground. Though Al was clearly the winner and continued with the headlock, Mato's moves were impressive.

"Now, kid, say uncle." Al persisted.

At this point, Mato gasped for air and wanted to be done with this little show. He gruffly mumbled, "Uncle," ready to give up.

Al loosened his grip ever so slightly, "Louder, please."

"*Uncle*," Mato roared.

Al released Mato. They rose to their feet and touched muzzles. The other bears came over.

Ket slapped Mato on the back. "You got him to the ground, young bear. Impressive."

Oslo chimed in, "Yeah, but he still said, 'Uncle!'"

"All this excitement!" Sven exclaimed.

"And wrestling!" Lars added.

Slick did a fake boxing dance around the group. He stopped when he heard Mato and Al announce, "We are *hungry!*"

All the other bears nodded in agreement.

Mato asked, "But, Al, how are all seven of us going to eat? We can't keep hanging out—we are going to have to go on our own and hunt—"

"I don't know, kid," Al said. "You might see a bunch of bears along a carcass together."

"Maybe," Mato started. This conversation had caught the full attention of the other bears, "Well, maybe we can find a whale?"

Ket chimed in, "Fat chance to find a beached whale—no beach, silly boy!"

"Yeah, bears only eat in groups around a big ol' whale carcass, already dead!" Oslo added.

"Where is this whale?" Sven asked.

"Ya, I like whale!" Lars added. He and Sven kept nodding in agreement.

Mato asked, "What if it's not a carcass?"

"Just what are you saying kid?" When Mato shrugged, Al kept talking, "I know there are white whales this far north. Maybe…nah," Al waved his paw and turned away.

Ket was curious, "What about white whale?"

Oslo chided, "Nothing, nothing about white whale, you can't just go and catch one—"

"Ya, ya!" Sven jumped up and down, "Hunt a white whale!"

"Ya, ya" Lars joined in the jumping up and down, "Have yummy dinner!"

Slick added, "There'd be plenty left over for me!"

Al looked at Mato, "OK, let me get this straight. You mean to tell me that this crew wants to go and hunt whale?"

Mato looked at the others, "Do you guys? You want to catch a white whale?"

Oslo and Ket looked at each other, then at Sven, Lars, and now Slick jumping up and down. They all replied, "Yes, ya, yep!"

Al said, "Well, kid, I guess it's settled then. We are having whale for supper."

Mato nodded, "I'm sure glad you guys came up with this idea."

Oslo and Ket shook front paws, Sven and Lars hugged each other, and Slick began pacing again.

Chapter Sixteen

A WHALE OF A PLAN

Al led the group to an area along the coast where there was more pack ice and some ice floes. Mato remembered seeing the white whales once when he was with Nana and Ursula. The whales traveled together and came up to the surface of the water for air, like seals. But, unlike the seal, they usually stayed in groups.

Mato had no idea how they were going to get one away from its group, not to mention capturing one. He caught up to Al and asked, "How are we going to find a white whale alone?"

"Well," Al explained, "If we have timed this right, there is usually a pod or two that passes this way. If we are lucky, one might get trapped by a floe and the edge of the ice shore. Or…" Al quickly turned around.

"Where are you going?" Mato asked. The other bears stopped and watched as Mato and Al walked away from the sea. Al turned to the bears and shouted, "Watch the waterline for a pod of white whales, could be a group as small as ten or as big as fifty!" he turned to Mato, "Come with me, kid, we are going to look for a whale-sized air hole."

Al padded along swiftly with his nose close to the ice. He stopped so abruptly that Mato bumped into him. "Here, kid, look." Al pointed to a break in the ice that was about four feet wide and twenty feet long.

"A whale-sized air hole!" Mato shouted.

"OK, kid, time to figure out how to make this happen." Al turned and headed back to the ocean.

Al and Mato rejoined the other bears scanning the ocean for a sign of the white whales.

Al explained to them, "Sometimes a whale swims under the edge of the ice along the waterline, thinking it's just an ice floe, and comes up for air along the way. When it sees it swam too far inland, it keeps using the same air hole to figure out what to do. A whale can panic and wear itself out. That's when we have our chance. Slick, you are our lookout."

Slick nodded and started pacing at the edge of the pack ice, nervously observing the water's edge.

"Oslo, you're my runner, as soon as Slick says he sees a pod, run to get us ready at the air hole."

Oslo stood up onto two legs and saluted Al, "Can do, sir!"

Al had turned toward Ket already, but glanced back at Oslo, "At ease." Al proceeded, "Mato, Ket, Sven, and Lars—the five of us will make the grab."

Mato was amazed at how quickly this was coming together, that the Spirit Bear was right about the white whale, and that Al knew what to do. He asked Al, "Have you done this before?"

Al started to lead the group to the air hole, "Not even once, kid."

Now Mato was concerned.

The five bears relaxed near the air hole and discussed their plan. And they waited. Mato was used to waiting around during a hunt. So much of hunting was waiting and timing, it was essential for a bear to have patience. While Mato waited for his prey to appear, he liked to visualize the capture. That way when the moment came to take action, Mato felt like he was in a zone. It was a way to be in the stillness and quiet before he could pounce. The bears had agreed to let the whale come up at least once to see which direction it faced and then they would stealthily move into position.

Al volunteered to be the distraction. Sven and Lars would attack first, as they were the quickest. Then Mato and Ket would add their strength to get the whale completely out of the water. The bears knew that, like with a seal, they had no chance in the water with the whale, but on top of the ice they could subdue their prey.

Mato was impressed with the quiet patience of these male bears, especially Sven and Lars who always seemed wiggly and silly. He could tell that when it came to the hunt, these bears were not playing.

Sven picked up his head as though he had heard something, and all five quietly rose to their feet. They could hear Slick's shouts, then silence. Slick had shouted to Oslo, and Oslo gave the signal. But he soon became silent so as not to disturb the hunt. Oslo waited for Slick to catch up to him, and then they padded closer to watch the rest of the bears complete the mission.

A massive white head emerged from the water. The animal made a swooshing sound, spouting water out and taking air in through its blowhole. Once the whale submerged again, the bears moved in closer to take their positions. They knew it could be several minutes before the whale surfaced again. Sven and Lars steadied themselves.

A few minutes later, the bears saw air bubbles rising. Al waved his arms to get the whale's attention. The whale could not reverse his upward propulsion upon seeing Al. At the height of its extension out of the water, Sven and Lars dove at the whale across the ice opening. In one sweeping motion, they pushed his head toward the edge of the opening as Mato and Ket pounced to help propel the whale fully onto the surface. The four of them managed to keep the whale out of the water as Al joined in for the kill.

The bears dragged the whale carcass away from the air hole. They started eating the whale, not even observing hunt etiquette, allowing Oslo to join right in for the meal. Slick paced and waited for the scraps. He liked to clean up the leftovers.

CHAPTER SEVENTEEN

SLICK'S STORY

The male bears lounged for several days after their white whale hunt. The meal was enough to satisfy them for well over a week. They had wandered further along the ocean, and settled near an ice floe area with several pockets of water.

Mato swam every day. He enjoyed the water. He even played games with Sven and Lars. He enjoyed playing King of the Ice Floe. The king was whoever lasted the longest without being pushed into the water. Mato always let the other two push him in first. Then he would swim around and watch Sven and Lars wrestle.

The pair would often fall into the water together because they were so busy wrestling that they didn't pay attention to where the edge was. Sven and Lars wrestled even underwater until they had to come up for air. Still entwined, they would surface together for a breath then continue their joust.

Mato also enjoyed challenging Sven and Lars to see who could stay under the longest. Mato was good at staying under; one of the few games he played better than his sister did.

Oslo and Ket liked to take bets on who would surface first. They would eventually break even because there was a different winner each time. Under the water, Sven and Lars often tickled Mato, which caused him to laugh and surface early. Sven and Lars would sometimes tickle each other with the same result.

Mato noticed that Slick barely spent time in the water. He finally had the patience to ask him about it, as conversations with Slick could be confusing. "Slick, why don't you swim more?" Mato asked the pacing bear.

Slick stopped for a moment, "'Cause I'm Slick—look at me, my fur ain't right!" He started pacing again.

"Yeah," Mato persisted, "about that. What happened to your fur?" He settled in, hoping to get some answers from Slick's ramblings.

"Used to *love* swimming! Loved it! Shoot, damn humans, ruined my Alaska, wrecked my home, my coast, my water, my hunting...Good dumps though, yeah...they got the dumps..." He stopped and looked at Mato, "You see the dump?"

Mato shook his head. "Swimming," he reminded Slick.

"Yeah, well, I swam right into it! The human waste...their big oil machine on the water broke and I swam right in it!" He paced.

Mato had to ask, "Swam in what?"

Slick stopped again, "Oil! Swam in oil! It don't mix with water! *No*, sir—it's not good for my coat!"

Mato thought to himself, "Oil...I'll bet he's talking about the black gold the Spirit Bear said drove him out of Alaska. He also remembered Slick mentioning the Big Spill.

"Had to leave! Leave home!" Slick stood up on his hind legs and waved his paws around. "Good-bye, Alaska!" Slick hollered. Then he began to mutter, "Found the dump, found it, yeah, found the dump..." He dropped back to all fours and paced.

Mato figured that would be the most information he could get from Slick, so he wandered over to the others to see if they knew more about the whole oil thing.

Mato still wasn't sure he knew what oil was. Oslo saw him and said, "What are ya doing to poor old Slick?"

Mato sat down by Oslo, "I asked him why he didn't swim very much. Hey, Oslo, what is the deal with this oil stuff? Is it also called *black gold*?"

Oslo chuckled, "Black gold? Where did ya hear that? Yeah, black gold, oil, sludge…humans are crazy for it."

"Why?" asked Mato.

"See here, kid, I have a theory," Oslo explained, "I think they use that stuff to make all their machines work. Every time I've been near the humans, I could smell the stuff."

Mato faintly remembered a strange smell when the whirlybird landed with Umky. He figured that was what a whirlybird smelled like. The humans had their own smell, but the machine smell was completely different. "Why was it in the water?"

"That my friend," Oslo shifted closer to Mato, "is what they call a spill." He leaned back and crossed his front paws across his chest, satisfied with how much he knew about oil.

"Is that the Big Spill?" Mato prodded, referring to Slick.

"The *biggest*! Oh, it spilled out of a water machine, a really big one, like the oil came right out of it. That big machine stayed in one place on the surface of the water and had a big pointy thing sticking out of it, taller than an iceberg. The boat machines would go up next to it and take oil away. Except this time, it shot oil out onto the water! It spread across the water for miles, blocking the Alaskan tundra. As a matter of fact, that's how our buddy got his name, Slick. That's what the oil on the water is called. Our man swam through it…probably inhaled some. I think that's why he's not quite right. That oil and the dump did something to him.

"We had him tagging along after Churchill. It was weird how he didn't want to hunt or even eat. Then Ket said to tell him that the leftovers were the dump. It fooled him the first time. Al's been letting him eat scraps ever since. Slick just followed along; happy to have whatever we left for him. As you can see, he really doesn't eat much. I'm surprised he's even alive. With his messed up fur and little blubber, you'd think the first blizzard would do him in; but not our buddy Slick. He's really the toughest bear I've ever seen. I think these big fellas would agree."

Ket and Al, supposedly sleeping, grunted their agreement.

Mato looked over at Slick. "Thanks, Oslo that explains a lot."

Oslo blushed and puffed himself up. "Even a small bear knows a thing or two!"

Ket and Al groaned. Mato laughed and looked up at the sky. Nana's star twinkled. Mato was glad to be among these male bears. Sure, they could be dangerous if they wanted to, but the way that they let Slick hang around made him feel proud to be in their company. As the star shone brighter, Mato began to wonder if Nana had orchestrated his first encounter with these bears. Mato knew that she hadn't done anything by accident. He noticed the other star twinkling near Nana's. Of course she knew the Spirit Bear. Nana knew everything. She especially knew to let her son learn about certain things from somewhere else. It made his memories of his mother and sister that much sweeter. He sighed and, with a big grin, fell asleep.

Chapter Eighteen

FISHY WHALES

While lounging on an ice floe, Mato noticed Sven and Lars playing near the edge of the water. They weren't wrestling, but circling and bouncing a few feet away from each other. Mato was curious about this new game they were playing and slid into the water to get a closer look. As he approached them, Mato could see that Sven and Lars were each holding some sort of stick.

"Take that!" shouted Sven.

"No, you take that!" volleyed Lars.

"What are you two up to?" Mato asked as he climbed out of the water.

Sven and Lars pointed their weapons at Mato, "Take that!" They shouted. Without flinching, Mato sniffed at the sticks. "Where did you get those?"

"Just over there," said Sven, pointing with his stick beyond a nearby ridge.

"Ya, there," chimed in Lars as he flipped his stick around, clashing it against the one Sven held. They began playing again.

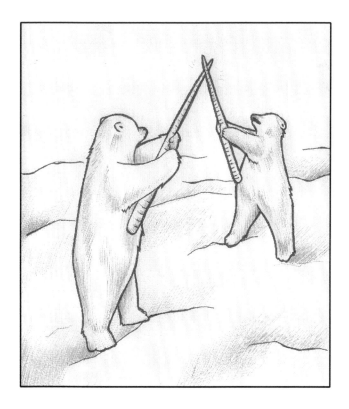

Mato shouted, "Guys!" Sven and Lars paused, looking at Mato, who then calmly continued, "Can you show me where you got them?"

"Ya sure," Sven said dropping his stick.

"Come with us," Lars started walking with his stick and Sven slapped it away from him. This started a slapping fight between them.

"Guys!"

Sven and Lars laughed as they led Mato to where they found the sticks. Just over the ridge and along the shore, the ice pack had formed into a small harbor. At the edge of the ocean, there was a large expanse of water without ice. As they got closer, Mato could see something bobbing up and down in the water. He saw the sticks that Sven and Lars had been playing with. "What are those?" Mato asked Sven and Lars.

"We call them fishy whales." Sven replied.

"Ya, they is fishy, but whale."

Mato looked at them puzzled.

"Ya! Come, boy, smell…" Lars urged.

Mato nosed the air, "I guess they do smell a little like fish. I think they smell more like the white whales. How did you get their sticks? Did you hunt them?"

"Nah, no hunt," Sven said.

"Yah, too big," Lars continued.

"We found sticks lying around," Sven finished.

"How big are these whales?" Mato asked wondering if it was the unicorn whale that the Spirit Bear spoke about.

"Big as white whale," Sven and Lars answered simultaneously. They looked at each other and laughed. As they finished laughing, they turned to look at Mato. "Hey!" They shouted.

"We know what you are thinking, young bear," Sven said.

"You want to hunt fishy whale," Lars said, pushing Mato.

Mato smiled, "You guys wait here while I go get the others."

Sven and Lars held their positions observing the fishy whales as Mato left.

"Hey Sven, you think you will like fishy whale?" Lars asked.

"Ya, ya, I do—I think it will be like kelp covered white whale!" Sven replied.

"Oh, ya, seaweed kind of fishy," Lars agreed.

The two continued discussing the delicacies of their arctic menu while awaiting Mato's return.

Mato picked up one of the sticks that the Danes had been playing with. He approached the lounging bears, passing the pacing Slick.

Oslo lifted his head as Mato approached with the stick in his mouth. "Watcha got there kid?"

Mato dropped the stick to the ground beside Oslo and Ket. Ket rolled over to look.

"Ah," Ket noticed. "Must be narwhal (nar -WALL) close."

Mato and Oslo looked at each other, then at Ket, "Narwhal?"

Ket grunted. "And this," he said holding up the stick, "is tusk."

Al, who slumbered nearby stirred a little. Oslo shook his head, "OK, big guy, are ya gonna tell us what it is or not?"

Ket pushed himself up to a seated position and reached for the stick. He examined it as he spoke, "Narwhal is whale. Like white whale, they are together, but none leave the group for an air hole like white whale. Narwhal are always together bobbing up and down. You see them, then you don't see them. They come and go."

"Can you hunt them?" Mato asked.

"Eh, too many, like trying to catch walrus, they poke you with the big teeth thing." He explained jabbing at Mato with the stick. "But good meal, like most whales, if you find dead one."

At this point, Al turned over. He moved from his back to his side. He propped his head up with a front paw resting his elbow on the snow and stated plainly, "Looks like we have a new hunt fellas."

Mato nodded, "Sven and Lars are already on the lookout."

Al stretched and rose to all fours, "Lead the way, kid."

Slick noticed the four bears pass him, paced a few more times, and decided to follow.

Mato asked Ket, "Is this narwhal also known as a unicorn whale?"

Ket replied, "I have heard this, but don't know what unicorn is. They are narwhal."

Mato was satisfied that a narwhal was indeed the unicorn whale the Spirit Bear talked about, even if they didn't know what a unicorn was.

Sven and Lars were still chatting about the taste of things when the other bears arrived. "Oh, hey!" They said, finally noticing Mato had returned with the others.

"Did young bear tell you?" Sven asked.

"He wants to hunt fishy whale!" Lars added.

"Narwhal," Ket corrected.

Sven and Lars tried to sound out this new word, "Nare-no-whale-wall." They looked at each other and agreed, "Ya, fishy whale."

Ket rolled his eyes and joined in the observation of their new prey.

The bears waited for Al to speak. They could tell that he was coming up with a strategy for the hunt.

He pointed to the group of narwhals. "We could try to get one to…no, wait, no, that won't work. We can approach by land and wait—no. Hmmm, we can go under the nearest ice floe and…OK fellas—I have a plan!"

Apparently, Al had not always been asleep the past few weeks. He had noticed that Sven, Lars, and Mato had spent a considerable amount of time in the water and their games had improved their underwater diving skills. He assigned the three of them to approach the group of narwhals from beneath the nearby ice sheet. They would have to single out one of the strange whales from beneath the surface to attempt to separate it. Polar bears could be just as stealth underwater as on land, and the three of them had practiced these moves challenging each other through play. Al knew that he and Ket were the stealthiest on land, and that Oslo was the most agile. He needed Oslo to take hold of the tusk and keep it out of the way. Al also knew that Slick could pace on an ice floe upwind from the narwhals to keep them aware of a bear nearby while distracting them from the hunt above and below the surface.

Luckily, there was an ice floe on three sides of the narwhals. Even if the pod made its escape, the bears would not be approaching from that direction. The entire plan was to focus on one whale, and ignore the rest. Al quickly gave each bear his assignment.

Slowly and silently, the bears moved into position. Because the ice floe wasn't too thick, Al, Oslo, and Ket could sense Sven, Lars, and Mato underneath. The above bears distributed their weight evenly, so as not to break through the ice and draw the narwhals' attention. They could see Slick pacing on the opposite ice floe, and they felt the narwhals move toward them, closer to their edge. Timing was everything, as the three bears under the water chose one whale for attack.

Sven, Lars, and Mato did not want to get caught in the cluster of creatures, so they picked one bobbing closest to the ice floe. As the narwhal moved toward the surface, all three bears came from underneath it and forced the narwhal upward. There was splashing and panic among the other whales. Mato felt a jab in his side, but he kept focused on his task. Al and Ket continued the whale's propulsion out of the water and onto the ice flow while Oslo wrapped himself around the tusk. Sven, Lars, and Mato scrambled out of the water. Though most of the narwhals moved away from the commotion, several remained in the area and jabbed at the bears.

The ice floe was breaking apart so the bears had to move quickly to get their catch to the edge of the ice shore. With that many bears, the whale was moved to the shore in seconds. As the bears began eating their meal along the shore, the lingering narwhals joined the rest of their pod and swam out to sea.

Mato quickly examined his side. He could see where the tusk had broken his black skin through to the blubber, but that was as far as it went. He considered himself lucky since those tusks were long enough to go all the way through him! He joined the other bears in the feast.

CHAPTER NINETEEN

TAGGED

"Help! Help! Help! Help!" Lars broke the lounging silence of the group with his screams. The male bears hadn't moved much since dining on narwhal several days ago, and were enjoying a good rest.

"Wake up! Wake up! Wake up!" Lars shook Mato, then Oslo. Ket and Al growled loudly before Lars got to them.

"They have Sven, they have Sven, please, please come *now*!"

Mato and Oslo tried to calm Lars, "Breathe, ya big Dane, breathe!" shouted Oslo.

Mato asked calmly, "Who has Sven?"

"The humans! Humans have him! Come, come quickly!" He tried to pull Mato with him by his front paw.

Now Al and Ket became interested. They nodded to each other, stood on two legs, and walked to either side of Lars. Mato wriggled his front paw free and moved away.

Lars frantically looked back and forth from Ket to Al pleading, "Please, we have to save him."

Al and Ket shook their heads and gently sat Lars down.

Oslo repeated more quietly, "That's it, Dane, breathe. Just breathe."

Lars heaved a few inhales and exhales and Mato gently suggested, "Now, tell us exactly what happened."

They all listened closely as Lars explained, "We were exploring like we always do, being silly...playing, you know," he nervously looked at the others, "when I went to run so Sven could chase me, ya? So, I ran, and ran, but no Sven, he always catches me, you know." The other bears nodded and Lars continued, "I looked back to see him surrounded by *humans*! Then he fell to ground and humans moved in on him! I ran all the way here!" Lars became agitated and tried to stand up. Al and Ket held him down. "Pleeeeze! We have to save him!" Lars cried.

"We will," Mato calmly assured him, "But we have to be really careful!"

Al strategized while still holding Lars, "Mato, you and Oslo are going to have to go. Ket and I will stay here with Lars. He's too hysterical and will get us all into trouble."

"But I know where they are!" Lars protested.

"Just point us in the direction," Oslo reassured him, "We'll bring your boy back!"

Lars pointed, "Go! Go now, that way! Hurry!"

Al reached for Mato, "Kid, go tell Slick to stand lookout, in case those humans are headed our way."

Mato nodded, sprinted over to Slick, and then sprinted in the direction Lars had pointed. Oslo caught up with Mato.

Slick came over to Al, Ket, and Lars, "They going to the dump?"

Lars crumbled into tears, wailing loudly.

"Keep an eye out would ya, Slick?" Al asked, "And let me know when Oslo or Mato come back."

"Sure thing," Slick replied. Slick may not be "right" as Oslo pointed out, but he was a reliable look out. Al figured he learned that trick from all the sneaking around human dumps.

Mato and Oslo moved swiftly in the direction Lars had pointed. They came up to a low ridge and slowed to sniff the air. They had a strong scent of Sven.

Oslo asked Mato, "You picking up anything other than Sven?"

"Yeah," replied Mato, "But it's pretty faint."

"Me too, kid. My guess is he's been tagged," Oslo said.

Mato thought back to the thing in Umky's ear, and the scents around him then. He hoped getting tagged was all that happened to Sven. Mato didn't think Lars would survive without his partner. Sure, it was strange, but those two were inseparable. They were like one polar bear in two bodies. They completed each other.

Oslo sensed Mato's concern. "Don't worry, kid; we'll have those lovebirds reunited as soon as the stun wears off of Sven."

Mato sniffed the air again. He wondered if the faint smell was from oil. It didn't smell like any creature he hunted, but was kind of mixed with a mammal odor. "Is *that* what you mean by an oil smell?" he asked.

"Sure is," said Oslo. "It's probably why it is fading so fast, because they have those machines that move quickly on the snow."

"I've only seen a whirlybird," Mato explained.

"Best to keep it that way," Oslo assured him.

They moved quietly and cautiously onward as the scent from Sven became stronger. Oslo spotted Sven, and signaled to Mato without a sound. Mato nodded and the two became even stealthier, as though approaching prey. With each step, they checked the air to be sure the other faint smell had not become stronger. The other scent had faded in a way that made the bears almost certain that the humans had moved on in the opposite direction from where they came.

Moving closer, they heard Sven's short breaths. Mato and Oslo sighed with relief that their friend was alive. They went over to Sven so that he could see them. Sven was motionless, except for the movements of his breathing. Oslo and Mato saw the fear in Sven's eyes quickly change to relief as they came into his view. Sven was aware enough to recognize them. Mato gently touched the tag on Sven's ear with his muzzle. Sven blinked.

"I'll run and tell the others, you stay here with him," Oslo said.

Mato nodded and settled in beside Sven, so that Sven could still see him while Oslo trotted away. Mato touched the tag on Sven's ear again and said, "You know Lars is going to want one of these too."

Sven breathed louder and faster. Now his eyes were smiling.

CHAPTER TWENTY

REUNITED

Whed Oslo got close enough that Slick could hear him he called out, "It's safe! Sven is OK!" He saw Slick hustling to let the others know.

Lars struggled to free himself from Al and Ket. Slick told them Sven was OK. But Al and Ket would not let Lars free until they could see Oslo for themselves and heard him repeat, "It's safe! Sven is OK!" Then they let Lars loose.

Lars bowled over Slick, pushing him to the ground. Slick lay there and groaned. Lars then bounded past Oslo, who started to say something but decided not to. Lars was far past him within seconds.

Oslo met up with the others, "Sven has been tagged. Mato stayed with him since he still can't move, but we could tell he recognized us."

Al and Ket started walking, Oslo helped Slick back to his feet. Al muttered, "Terrific, all that time in bear jail, none of us got tagged. *Now* that silly Dane will attract and bring the humans around!"

"Way out here on ice," Ket added. He and Al casually walked in the direction that Lars ran. Oslo and Slick rested for a minute before following along.

Mato entertained Sven with the story about finding Umky and the purpose of Umky's ear tag. Sven woke up enough to speak, "I wonder what the humans want? I hope they will give me treats like in zoo." He moved his head a little, "Lars must be so sad and worried."

"That's an understatement! Al and Ket had to hold him down, in case the humans were still here!" Mato exclaimed.

Just as Sven started to laugh he was pummeled by Lars. Mato jumped aside and watched.

"Sven! Sven! Sven! Speak to me, ya? Sven!" Lars lay on top of Sven holding his head in both front paws and shouting in his face.

"Ya, ya, get off me, ya!" Sven said loudly to Lars.

Lars leapt off Sven and knelt by his side, investigating every inch of Sven's body. Lars lifted Sven's front paw, then let it fall. He did the same with the other three. "Sven, you are like kelp, no?" Lars observed.

Sven laughed, "Ya, Lars, I am seaweed bear!"

Lars laughed and then threw his front paws out and buried his head in Sven's chest and sobbed.

Sven looked over Lars's head toward Mato, "We have never been apart. We are twins, from same momma. She was very young. She had no idea what to do with us! She stayed long as she could, then we were on our own. We took care of each other."

Mato could barely hear Sven over the sobbing Lars. But Mato understood growing up close to a sibling and spending every moment together, only to leave and maybe never see one another again. Sven and Lars had a special relationship. Maybe the only polar bear one of its kind. It was unique in the Arctic for two cubs to grow up together, *never* to separate, and to survive. In fact, it was unheard of! Again, Mato felt honored to be in the company of this group of bears.

Lars suddenly stopped crying and sat up, looking at Sven, who was able to move his head a little. "Sven! What is that lovely thing in your ear?" Mato and Sven laughed.

"What? What so funny?" Lars crossed his front paws.

"That," Mato explained, "Is his tag."

Lars pawed at Sven's tag as Sven started to wiggle his paws. Lars screeched, "I *must* have it!" He started to gnaw at Sven's ear.

Sven squirmed, "Ah! You tickle me! Ah!" Sven was getting his motion back quickly. He reached a front paw around and put Lars in a headlock, pulling him down beside him.

The two bears rolled back and forth on top of each other. Lars shouted, "I *want* tag!" And Sven wailed in response, "It is my ear!"

Mato stood up to see Al and Ket approaching. The three of them shook their heads and watched the brothers wrestle some more.

Al commented, "I see these lovebirds are doing OK."

"You know what tag means." Ket reminded.

"Not right now, Ket," Al said. "Let's relax here, the humans are gone, and I'm still sleeping off the last hunt." He settled in for a nap.

Mato looked at Ket, "*What* does the tag mean?"

Ket looked back at Mato as he too settled for a nap, "Tag means humans come back."

Mato looked at Sven and Lars as they wrestled, with grunting instead of arguing.

"Yeah," Al sighed. "I'm gonna miss them Danes."

Mato slowly moved to lie on his belly, resting his head, and still watching Sven and Lars. He realized that Oslo and Slick would still be coming and he stood up to greet them. Mato did not like the tone of Ket and Al. So, he asked Oslo as he and Slick approached.

"Oslo," Mato asked, "do you have to stay away from tagged bears?"

"Only if you want to stay away from humans," Oslo replied.

"Dang," said Slick. "I'm gonna miss them Dane dudes."

Mato settled in right there to nap. He thought about Umky and his tag. He thought about how Umky didn't stay around very long after the hunt. He figured his uncle was protecting him from humans. After all, Umky was tagged. He had become some sort of human zoo experiment. Mato hoped that Sven would not have to go to the zoo but, if he did, that the humans would take Lars as well. After being around these bears all this time and seeing Sven and Lars together, he couldn't imagine them apart.

Chapter Twenty-One

RIGHT WHALE

None of the bears wanted to part from Sven and Lars. They were useful in the new hunting efforts. After much discussion, they all decided that after the next hunt Sven and Lars would move to another location. Meanwhile, they stayed near the ocean, keeping an eye out for any type of meal.

Slick spotted something out on the water. He thought it was a boat and he got excited that there might be humans on it. This caught the attention of the other bears who looked up just as the object went below the surface. Now they thought Slick was seeing things. It wouldn't be the first time. As the others put their heads back down, Mato kept watching. The object surfaced again, moving closer to the shore where the bears gathered.

"Whoa!" Mato breathed out as he stood up to join Slick.

"You see it too, right?" Slick asked.

"Yeah," Mato moved closer to Slick and the shore.

"That ain't no boat, I can see it now," Slick explained. "And I've even seen a human boat that comes up out of the water, but it don't do it as quick as this."

"No," Mato said, "I've never seen any of those things, but my Nana did tell me about a really big sea whale, maybe that's what it is."

Ket heard the mention of whale and decided to have a look. Of everyone in the group, he was the most knowledgeable about whales. "Ah," Ket confirmed, "I have seen this. Big whale came to die when I was cub in Siberia. Many bears came and ate for days. They called it bowhead whale."

Mato was awestruck, "There is no way that even seven of us can catch something *that* big!"

Ket laughed, "You don't kill whale, big bowhead whale. Bowhead come to shore to die. Hmm, this is strange. We are on ice, whale die on land."

The three of them watched the whale swim closer as the other bears slowly gathered. Sven and Lars jumped up and down each time the whale breached the surface. It was quite a show to see it spewing water from its blowhole as it rose out of the water. The whale just kept coming closer and closer.

"That's as big as a boat!" Slick exclaimed.

The whale busted an ice floe apart as it got closer and with its last breach out of the water, it hurled itself onto the shelf of the ice shore. The bears jumped back so as not to get hit by the rush of flying ice, snow, and water. Sven and Lars were too excited to be cautious and ran through the debris over to the whale. They were pushed aside by its tail.

As the other bears gathered, the whale spoke in a Portuguese accent, "I am Alma, from Mozambique." She boomed. She shuddered as she continued, "I am from where the oceans are warm and the shores have sand. I am far from my home. My kind is Right Whale. It is our custom to listen for the call of the shore where we are meant to die. I have been called to this cold, very cold, place." She shuddered again. "I have been told that the sea bear needs my nourishment." Her voice had a high-pitched echo quality to it.

Oslo, Ket, and Al sat down like bear cubs ready to listen to a story from their mother. Mato and the others continued to stand on two legs, stunned and open-mouthed.

Alma shuddered again and sighed. Her large eye scanned the group of polar bears, "You look like the sea bears, the hungry white bears of the north."

Sven and Lars started dancing and singing, "Ya, we are sea bears, sea bears, ya!"

Alma shot a stream of water from her blowhole that landed directly on Sven and Lars, "Listen to me very carefully!" She warned. "I am here for a greater purpose, much bigger than just the seven of you. You must follow *all* of my instructions. You are the seven to help me nourish the multitude."

The bears looked at each other. The rest sat down, even Sven and Lars. Alma continued, "I can only say this once, so *listen* carefully and no questions or interruptions! There is little time before I die."

"You will know I am dead when the air is gone from me. There will not be a sound from my blowhole. When the sound has ceased for one hour, I will be gone. Wish me well upon my new journey, but *do not feast* yet. You are to wait three full days after my death. There will be no feast for the seven until the multitudes have gathered. You are to move away from this body and allow the many to feast upon me.

"The three days lets my scent reach many who will come. I am gathering the sea bears of the future: the females, who will need nourishment so they can den in the winter and bear their young; the cubs, who need to grow strong; and the weary males, who need to be nourished so they will not prey on their own to survive. There is plenty for all, and you are the seven to make sure all are nourished. After three more days, you may have your fill of my bounty." Alma shuddered again, and then sighed, "Questions?"

Lars, "Do you taste fishy?" Sven smacked him.

Alma ignored them. She looked at Al. Mato nudged Al, who cleared his throat, "Great Alma, on behalf of all sea bears, I thank you for your willingness to endure our cold climate in your final days."

The other bears, including Sven and Lars bowed to her.

Mato added, "Thank you for taking such good care of yourself so we can have such bounty!"

Al looked at him, then continued "Yeah, OK, well Great Alma, just to be certain…when your blowhole stops for an hour we wait three days for the other bears to gather and begin feasting and then three more days to start feasting ourselves?"

"That is correct, Alpha." Alma confirmed, "And while the others gather, it is up to you to see that the weaker are protected from the stronger. Make it understood that there is plenty for all."

Al spoke to the other bears, "Are you listening fellas? Alma has given us the honor of being in charge to be certain that no bear is harmed, especially females and cubs, by hungry bears eager to feast." The other six nodded and grunted in agreement.

Mato couldn't resist asking, "How do you know his name?"

Alma replied, "'Twas a twinkling star that led me here, Mato."

Mato and Al fell into each other and simultaneously said, "Nana!" They looked up and saw the star twinkle brightly.

Alma's breathing began to slow, and she seemed to be getting sleepy. "Remember," she said drifting off, "Peace unto you, and keep peace among sea bears."

The bears waited to hear more. After a few moments, Slick moved over to Alma and stood up on his hind two legs placing his forepaws against her, "Peace, Great Alma," he said, and pressed the side of his face against her.

One by one the other bears came and put a paw on Alma's side repeating, "Peace." They curled up beside her to wait for her last breath. Slick remained standing in the same position as if hugging the great whale.

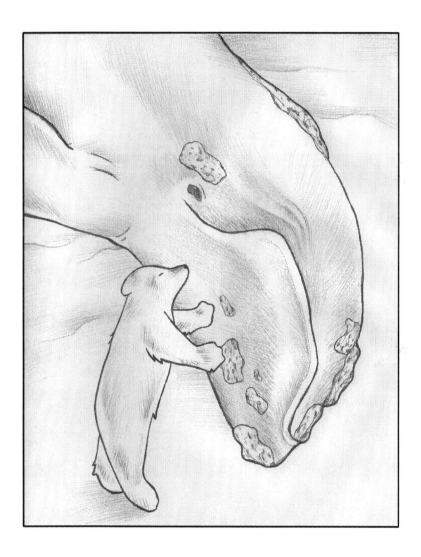

CHAPTER TWENTY-TWO

FINAL BREATH

A very different looking Slick removed his paws from the silent Alma. He dropped to four paws and gently touched Mato and then Al with his muzzle. Several hours had passed since Alma last spoke. As Mato and Al looked up, Slick said quietly, "She's gone."

Mato looked up at Slick and blinked a couple of times. "Slick?" Mato wasn't sure who it was.

"The one and only," he replied.

"Slick!" Mato excitedly stood on all fours, "You're back to normal polar bear color! You've lost your oily sheen."

Slick looked down at himself, turning to see his behind, "Hey, yeah, I look pretty good don't I?"

Al slowly got up and sniffed at Slick, "You smell better too!"

"How about that! I'm a new bear." Slick seemed pleased as he turned to look back at Alma.

Mato nodded when Al said, "Guess she really is a *Right* Whale."

"She's been silent for over an hour now." Slick said sadly.

"We should get the others and find a good spot to wait and watch." Mato said. He walked toward Sven and Lars. Slick and Al went to wake Oslo and Ket.

They found a place along the icy crags of the shore where they were upwind of Alma, but they still had her in view. The formations shielded them from any approaching bears easily spotting them. The seven settled in to nap and wait, even Slick, who didn't pace. Mato noticed, "Hey, Slick…" he whispered.

"Yeah, Mato?"

"Are you OK? You never settle in like this." Mato observed.

Slick yawned, "Haven't felt this good since…well, since I got the name Slick."

This made Mato curious, "What was your first name?"

Slick looked up for a moment, "I'm not sure I remember, Bo…Bu—I think it was Bu-fert."

"Bu-fert?" Mato asked.

"Aw, dude, I think that's close anyway."

Oslo, who was listening, walked over and settled next to Mato and Slick. "I think you might be trying to say Beaufort (*BOW-fort*)."

Slick jumped up, "Dude, that's it! Beaufort! My name is Beaufort!"

Oslo added, "I'll bet you were named after the same waters where you became Slick."

"What do you mean?" Mato asked Oslo.

"North of Alaska, where Slick—excuse me, where Beaufort is from, is called the Beaufort Sea." He explained smugly.

Slick yawned again, "I like it." He settled in to sleep.

Mato decided to take the first watch to see if anyone came for Alma yet.

Late into the second day, Sven and Lars took the watch together. They were bored, and took turns harassing the other napping bears. They worked their way up to Al, who growled and hissed as they approached.

"Awwww, Al!" Sven inched closer.

"Sven and I are soooo hungry—we want to eat whale now, ya?" Lars pleaded. Al slowly sat up, and motioned for Sven and Lars to move in closer.

Al whispered, "Closer boys, I want to tell you a secret about the whale."

Sven and Lars could hardly contain themselves. They wiggled and giggled as they bowed their heads before Al. *Klunk!* With his front paws, Al quickly grabbed each bear and knocked their heads together. Then he put them in a headlock, holding one in each arm. "If I see either one of you within fifty yards of that whale then *I* will be feasting on the two of *you*! Got it?" He then let them go.

Sven and Lars bounced onto their bottoms in front of Al. They rubbed their heads where their heads had hit. "Jeesh, Al, we just joke," Sven whined.

"Ya, Al, why so grumpy? If you want to wrestle, just say so—play nice, ya?" Lars added.

Al rose to all fours and let out a deep, vibrating growl. Sven and Lars scurried away. Al lay back down on his side, watching Sven and Lars. The pair nervously glanced back at him.

Oslo couldn't resist commenting, "You'd think after listening to the whale speak those Danes would get smarter, more respectful."

Ket added, "Danes, eh-maybe, Greenlanders, no."

Mato moved away from the group and settled into a nap that he hoped would last until the other bears came.

CHAPTER TWENTY-THREE

ON THE THIRD DAY

"Psst, psst!" Mato heard a tiny sound upwind from him. "Master Mato, psst!" Mato rose quietly to investigate, he did not want to disturb the other bears. This tiny voice was somehow familiar. "Charles?" Mato whispered.

The tiny fox popped his head up for Mato to see.

"Charles!" Mato exclaimed with a loud whisper. "What a nice surprise! I mean, it is a pleasure to meet your acquaintance again." Mato bowed.

"Ah," Charles noted as he pranced out from behind his hiding place. He bowed low, "The pleasure is all mine, Master Mato." He stood upright and continued, excited, yet quietly, "I am here on behalf of your dear sister, Miss Ursula. We were wondering—"

"About the Great Whale?" Mato interrupted.

"Why yes, yes, the Great Whale. Should we expect any trouble?"

"Not at all my friend. I will escort you and Ursula to the feast personally. Just give me a minute to tell the others, I will be right back." Mato assured him.

"Others?" Charles asked.

"Yes, others, remember the males I spoke with the last days that Nana was with us?"

"Of course, they spoke of many things you had not yet heard of." Charles replied.

Mato chuckled, "yeah, right- that seems so long ago now. Well, you are not going to believe this but that whale is actually from a very warm place. She was led here by Nana's star!"

Now Charles snickered, "I must say Master Mato, little surprises me these days. Let me guess, she has left you and the other males in charge so the feast will be peaceful?"

Mato shook his head and headed over to the other bears.

Charles hopped back to his hiding place and awaited Mato's return.

Mato went over to Oslo, Ket, and Al to tell them that bears were beginning to arrive, and that he would be going down closer to the whale.

"We'll keep an eye on ya, kid." Oslo replied.

Mato drew closer to Al and said softly, "You may want to join me after a while; there is someone I'd like you to meet."

"Sure thing, kid," Al said rolling over away from Mato.

Mato returned to Charles and said in his full voice, no longer whispering, "Lead me to my sister, fox friend!"

Charles hesitated at first, "M-m-Master Mato, are you sure there is no trouble?"

Mato smiled, "I guarantee it."

"Off we go then," Charles trotted further upwind before bearing right back around toward the whale.

As they walked, Mato explained about Alma and her instructions.

"You'll have to repeat all of this for your sister." Charles recommended, "Allow me to tell her you are approaching so you don't get attacked. She is hyperalert these days."

"Very well then," Mato tried to sound British, like Charles, but wasn't very good.

"Ah," acknowledged Charles, "Mimicry, the highest form of flattery."

They proceeded a bit further when Charles stopped abruptly. "I'll be right back." Mato sat down to wait for the go-ahead to approach his sister. He didn't mind at all. He knew better than anyone did how ferocious she could be. Charles continued upwind again. Mato watched for him to return. Then he heard a screeching growl and Ursula was bounding straight for him.

"Sis, it's me!" Mato hollered, "It's me…Mato!" But, it was too late. Ursula had already tackled him and pinned him to the ground.

"Hey, bro," Ursula said from her perch on top of her brother, as if it were no big deal. Mato was so grateful that this little reunion was out of sight of the other males. How silly he must have looked pinned down by a bear a third of his size!

Mato caught his breath, "Hey, sis, I have lots to tell you."

Ursula let Mato up, "So do I…but first, about that whale—"

"Of course," Mato replied, "First things first, and feasting is always first. Follow me!" Mato and Ursula began to trot in the direction of the Great Whale. He explained everything about Alma. By this time, other bears-not of the seven bears-, strange bears, coming from miles away were approaching, so Mato explained to Ursula that there were seven bears, including himself, appointed by Alma, the Great Whale, to keep the peace. Mato also explained that he and the others still had to wait three more days to eat.

"I'm proud of you, bro!" Ursula commended Mato, "I guess I never needed to worry."

"Have your feast, sis," Mato gestured toward the whale. "Then we'll share stories before I have mine." He nodded in the direction of Charles's hiding place, "Be sure to bring some scraps to our friend."

Ursula faked her British accent, "Cheerio, dear brother, do come down from your lookout after I've had a proper meal."

Mato laughed, "Your accent has gotten better!" He headed toward the other bears on patrol.

Many bears came to eat from the whale. Some just sat and gnawed, while others dragged away huge chunks of blubber. Occasionally, a male would try to claim an entire section, but the seven bears took turns keeping the peace. Sometimes they would go in a group of four and simply approach the greedy male, which would cause him to instantly retreat. They wouldn't completely chase him away though. Al even threw some meat to a naughty male to let him know it was OK to eat, just not to get greedy.

Males, females, and some cubs still with their mothers continued to come to the feast. It was a polar bear celebration.

Chapter Twenty-Four

SIBLINGS

The day after Charles and Ursula appeared, Mato and Al approached a napping Ursula. Mato was about to make a sound to announce their approach when Ursula suddenly jumped at him. Mato retreated quickly, afraid of being pinned again in front of Al. Al, usually stern, could not stop laughing, "I missed out on so much as an only cub!"

"And who might you be?" Ursula hissed. She did not know this bear. Mato approached his sister again, "This is Nana's first son, Al, short for Alpha."

"Whoa," said Ursula. "I guess Nana was pretty old."

This time Mato was laughing. Al looked at him, "Very funny, kid. Like I said, I missed out being an only child."

"But seriously, sis, how have you been holding up?" Mato asked.

"I have to say it has been challenging. It seemed like another bear was always to the hunt before me, even other females. But we managed."

"We?" asked Al.

"Whoops, what's happening to me? It's usually Mato who slips up like that!" Ursula exclaimed.

"Don't worry. Al is OK and he knows about Nana and her foxes." Mato reassured her.

"And Mato still slips up all the time." Al added. "Well, Ursula, if you and the fox would like to stick around longer, we can teach you some new stuff we've learned. Your brother and I have managed to gather a hunting team. We are pretty good and eat very well."

"A hunting *team*?" Ursula asked incredulously, "That's unheard of!" Al and Mato looked at each other. Ursula added, "Wait, I do remember Spirit Bear telling you about the white whale—do you mean to tell me you can hunt white whale?" Mato and Al nodded. "That's a relief," Ursula added, "I wasn't sure if I'd get enough to eat to den for the entire winter."

"I see," Al said.

"See what?" Mato asked.

This time Al and Ursula looked at each other.

"*What?*" Mato shouted.

"Settle down, kid, I'll explain later. Why don't you catch up with your sister while we wait out the last day before our own feast?" Al suggested.

Mato groaned as Al and Ursula exchanged good-byes. "Fine," Mato grumbled, "Let's take a little walk so I can talk to Charles too...I've got an experience both of you are going to want to hear about." He was thinking about Umky, of course. "You can sleep more while I feast, then we'll let you in on the next hunt..."

Ursula started to walk, "OK, we'll go to Charles. As for that other stuff, we'll see..."

Charles was just finishing some whale meat Ursula had brought him. "Excuse me, while I clean up," he said as he rubbed his snout into the snow. He rolled about, stood up, and shook out his tiny body.

Mato laughed. He remembered how Charles always looked like a little snow puff after cleaning off.

"Har, har," Charles sniped as he combed down his tail and licked his paws. He finished and pranced up to Mato, "What stories do you have for us, Master Mato?"

"Aw, Charles, you don't have to call me Master Mato anymore. I'm grown up now and on my own," Mato pointed out.

"Very well then, Mato, do tell us your news." Charles sat down to listen.

Ursula jumped in, "Well, I just met our older brother, Alpha."

"Ah, yes," said Charles. "Nana had spoken of him, and so did the fox before me. He is Nana's firstborn, yes?"

Mato looked at Ursula, "Yeah." He turned back to Charles. "I'm also pretty certain that he is the one the Spirit Bear talked about. You know 'the one who came before me to show me about the white whale and the unicorn whale,'" Mato reminded them.

"What is a unicorn whale?" Ursula asked.

"You'll see one when we show you how we hunt as a team. It is actually called a narwhal. I'm guessing that is what he meant by a unicorn whale, because I still don't know what a unicorn is. But, that's not what I want to tell you about. I want to tell you that I met our uncle!" Mato couldn't hold the news back another second.

"Our uncle?" Ursula asked. "Oh! You met Nana's brother? Where? How? Isn't he in a zoo?"

"Not anymore. He even hunted with me!"

"Tell me, Mato," Charles began, "What was his name?"

"You are not going to believe this." Mato said, holding his paws in front of him. "Mato is his name."

"No way!" Ursula pushed Mato's shoulder with a front paw.

Mato repeatedly nodded his head, "*And*...he said that their mother, his and Nana's was called Ursula!"

This time Ursula stood up and pushed Mato back with both of her front paws. "No way!" she shouted.

Mato nodded his head while he stood back up. "I know! How cool is that?"

"Ahem." Charles said quietly. The bears turned to listen. "Your Nana loved you both so much that she named you after the most important bears in her life." He looked up at the sky. Mato and Ursula looked up, too. The three settled onto their backs and stared up at the glittering star.

"Did you tell Al about her?" Ursula asked Mato.

"Yeah, and he told me more about Umky." Mato replied.

"Umky?" Ursula turned to her brother.

"Yeah, Uncle Mato. He was given the name Umky at the zoo." Mato explained.

"Tell us more about him, Mato." Ursula urged him.

"Yes, do tell." Charles agreed.

For the rest of the day, Mato talked about Umky and his almost human encounters.

Chapter Twenty-Five

THE TEAM OF SEVEN

Most of the polar bears had wandered away by the end of the celebration's third day. A couple of mothers with cubs stayed nearby, as there was still plenty of whale left. A few hours into the next day, the seven went to have their feast. Slick, now Beaufort, said a few words before they started, "Thank you, Alma. I am now my true self, thanks to you. Slick was OK, but Beaufort is so much better!" All the others grunted and nodded in agreement, and each bowed before the carcass before eating.

A couple of hours after the seven had their fill and had napped, Ursula approached Mato. "Hey, bro, I'd better be going now."

Mato lifted his head, "But we want to show you how we team hunt! You and Charles need to stick around at least a few more days!" His loud yelling woke up the other six.

Oslo jumped to his feet and bowed, "Well hello, miss."

Ket grunted.

"Ah, such a pretty bear, ya?" Sven started.

"So petite and pretty, ya?" Lars finished.

Slick remained silent and watched.

Al growled, "Knock it off, boys. She's my little sister!" He moved in front of Ursula.

"Your *what?*" All five of them asked in unison.

"Our sister…" Mato began.

Oslo shook his head, "Will somebody please explain to me what the heck you guys are talking about?"

"Not twins like us, ya?" Sven asked.

"No," Lars answered, "Al is too old!"

"Enough!" Al shouted. "I was the first cub born to Nana, yes, Nanuqa." He started calm and slow. "Mato and Ursula are the last of her litters." He motioned toward his brother and sister. "Our Nana does not walk the ice, nor swim the water now. However, she is with us." He looked up at the star, as did Mato and Ursula.

Oslo and Ket looked up. Oslo said, "Oh, I get it. Your Nana is the star that led Alma here!"

"Whoa." said Ket.

Sven and Lars looked up, moved in a circle back to back until they were dizzy, and fell down. Lying on his back Sven shouted, "There! I see her star there!"

"Ya!" added Lars, "I see her too!"

Ursula asked Mato, "Are those two for real?"

All the males except for Sven and Lars replied, "You have no idea!"

Ursula chuckled, "And you expect me to think you all hunt as a team?"

"Yes ma'am!" Oslo said proudly.

"True. Two whale hunts now. White whale and narwhal," Ket added.

Ursula shook her head, "Unbelievable, now this I have to see."

"So you'll stick around?" Mato asked excitedly.

"If it's OK with the rest of team, sure. Like I said, I really want to see this team hunt. I mean *this* team hunt!" She pointed at all the bears.

Al laughed, "It's an unlikely bunch, but our brother has led us to this."

Mato blushed, "It's even more important that you learn too, Ursula. I realize now how much responsibility a female has."

"I appreciate that, Mato. Especially since this winter I'll be giving birth to cubs."

For several moments, for once, all the males were speechless.

The End

Or
The Beginning

Just the Facts

This story is a fable, filled with fantasy—like talking polar bears. However, quite a bit of research about polar bears, the Arctic, and the animals there went into the writing of this book. To learn more about polar bears, the Arctic, whales, and the Lakota language (used by Roland, the spirit bear), check out the websites below.

- For all things polar bear, including the latest research and ways that you can help to preserve the Arctic ice, go to: www.polarbearsinternational.org
- For information about right whales, beluga whales, narwhals, spirit bears and Arctic foxes go to: http://animals.nationalgeographic.com/animals/mammals/
- To learn more about the Lakota language used by the Spirit bear and ceremony go to: http://language.nativeweb.org/translation.htm

Read more adventures from the Arctic with Ursula in *North Star*, coming soon.

Made in the USA
Charleston, SC
12 June 2014